THE YOUNG MUSICIAN

OR,

FIGHTING HIS WAY

Horatio Alger

1st WORLD
LIBRARY
Literary Society

The Young Musician

Horatio Alger

© 1st World Library – Literary Society, 2004
PO Box 2211
Fairfield, IA 52556
www.1stworldlibrary.org
First Edition

LCCN: 2005901330

Softcover ISBN: 1-4218-1145-6
Hardcover ISBN: 1-4218-1045-X
eBook ISBN: 1-4218-1245-2

Purchase *"The Young Musician"*
as a traditional bound book at:
www.1stWorldLibrary.org/purchase.asp?ISBN=1-4218-1145-6

1st World Library Literary Society is a nonprofit organization dedicated to promoting literacy by:

- Creating a free internet library accessible from any computer worldwide.
- Hosting writing competitions and offering book publishing scholarships.

Readers interested in supporting literacy through sponsorship, donations or membership please contact:
literacy@1stworldlibrary.org
Check us out at: www.1stworldlibrary.ORG
and start downloading free ebooks today.

The Young Musician
contributed by Tim, Ed & Rodney
in support of
1st World Library Literary Society

CONTENTS

CHAPTER I.

A CANDIDATE FOR THE POORHOUSE.

"As for the boy," said Squire Pope, with his usual autocratic air, "I shall place him in the poorhouse."

"But, Benjamin," said gentle Mrs. Pope, who had a kindly and sympathetic heart, "isn't that a little hard?"

"Hard, Alrnira?" said the squire, arching his eyebrows. "I fail to comprehend your meaning."

"You know Philip has been tenderly reared, and has always had a comfortable home -"

"He will have a comfortable home now, Mrs. Pope. Probably you are not aware that it cost the town two thousand dollars last year to maintain the almshouse. I can show you the item in the town report."

"I don't doubt it at all, husband," said Mrs. Pope gently. "Of course you know all about it, being a public man."

Squire Pope smiled complacently. It pleased him to be spoken of as a public man.

"Ahem! Well, yes, I believe I have no inconsiderable

influence in town affairs," he responded. "I am on the board of selectmen, and am chairman of the overseers of the poor, and in that capacity I shall convey Philip Gray to the comfortable and well-ordered institution which the town has set apart for the relief of paupers."

"I don't like to think of Philip as a pauper," said Mrs. Pope, in a deprecating tone.

"What else is he?" urged her husband. "His father hasn't left a cent. He never was a good manager."

"Won't the furniture sell for something, Benjamin?"

"It will sell for about enough to pay the funeral expenses and outstanding debts-that is all."

"But it seems so hard for a boy well brought up to go to the poorhouse."

"You mean well, Almira, but you let your feelings run away with you. You may depend upon it, it is the best thing for the boy. But I must write a letter in time for the mail."

Squire Pope rose from the breakfast-table and walked out of the room with his usual air of importance. Not even in the privacy of the domestic circle did he forget his social and official importance.

Who was Squire Pope?

We already know that he held two important offices in the town of Norton. He was a portly man, and especially cultivated dignity of deportment. Being in easy circum-stances, and even rich for the resident of a village, he was naturally looked up to and credited with a worldly sagacity far beyond what he actually possessed.

At any rate, he may he considered the magnate of Norton. Occasionally he visited New York, and had been very much annoyed to find that his rural importance did not avail him there, and that he was treated with no sort of deference by those whom he had occasion to meet. Somehow, the citizens of the commercial metropolis never suspected for a single moment that he was a great man.

When Squire Pope had finished his letter, he took his hat, and with measured dignity, walked to the village post-office.

He met several of his neighbors there, and greeted them with affable condescension. He was polite to those of all rank, as that was essential to his retaining the town offices, which he would have been unwilling to resign.

From the post-office the squire, as he remembered the conversation which had taken place at the breakfast-table, went to make an official call on the boy whose fate he had so summarily decided.

Before the call, it may be well to say a word about Philip Gray, our hero, and the circumstances which had led to his present destitution.

His father had once been engaged in mercantile business, but his health failed, his business suffered, and he found it best-indeed, necessary - to settle up his affairs altogether and live in quiet retirement in Norton.

The expenses of living there were small, but his resources were small, also, and he lived just long enough to exhaust them.

It was this thought that gave him solicitude on his death-bed, for he left a boy of fifteen wholly unprovided for.

Let us go back a week and record what passed at the last interview between Philip and his father before the latter passed into the state of unconsciousness which preceded death.

"Are you in pain, father?" asked Philip, with earnest sympathy, as his father lay outstretched on the bed, his face overspread by the deathly pallor which was the harbinger of dissolution.

"Not of the body, Philip," said Mr. Gray. "That is spared me, but I own that my mind is ill at ease."

"Do you mind telling me why, father!"

"No; for it relates to you, my son, or, rather, to your future. When my affairs are settled, I fear there will be nothing left for your support. I shall leave you penniless."

"If that is all, father, don't let that trouble you."

"I am afraid, Philip, you don't realize what it is to be thrown upon the cold charities of the world."

"I shall work for my living," said Philip confidently.

"You will have to do that, I'm afraid, Philip."

"But I am not afraid to work, father. Didn't you tell me one day that many of our most successful men had to work their way up from early poverty!"

"Yes, that is true; but a boy cannot always get the chance to earn his living. Of one thing I am glad; you have a good education for a boy of your age. That is always a help."

"Thanks to you, father."

"Yes; though an invalid, I have, at all events, been able to give private attention to your education, and to do better for you than the village school would have done. I wish I had some relative to whom I might consign you, but you will be alone in the world."

"Have I no relatives?" asked Philip.

"Your mother was an only child, and I had but one brother."

"What became of him, father?"

"He got into trouble when he was a young man, and left the country. Where he went to I have no idea. Probably he went first to Europe, and I heard a rumor, at one time, that he had visited Australia. But that was twenty years ago. and as I have heard nothing of him since, I think it probable that he is dead. Even if he were living, and I knew where he was, I am not sure whether he would make a safe guardian for you."

"Have you any advice to give me, father?" asked

Philip, after a pause. "Whatever your wishes may be, I will try to observe them."

"I do not doubt it, Philip. You have always been an obedient son, and have been considerate of my weakness. I will think it over, and try to give you some directions which may be of service to you. Perhaps I may be able to think of some business friend to whom I can commend you."

"You have talked enough, father," said Philip, noticing his father's increasing pallor and the evident exertion with which he spoke. "Rest now, and to-morrow we can talk again."

Mr. Gray was evidently in need of rest. He closed his eyes and apparently slept. But he never awoke to consciousness. The conversation above recorded was the last he was able to hold with his son. For two days he remained in a kind of stupor, and at the end of that time he died.

Philip's grief was not violent. He had so long anti-cipated his father's death that it gave him only a mild shock.

Friends and neighbors made the necessary arrange-ments for the funeral, and the last services were performed. Then, at length, Philip realized that he had lost his best earthly friend, and that he was henceforth alone in the world. He did not as yet know that Squire Pope had considerately provided him with a home in the village poorhouse.

CHAPTER II.

PHILIP AT HOME.

"When the funeral was over, Frank Dunbar, whom Philip regarded as his most intimate friend, came up to him.

"Philip," he said, "my mother would like to have you spend a few days with us while you are deciding what to do."

"Thank you, Frank!" answered Philip. "But until the auction I shall remain at home. I shall soon enough be without a home."

"But it will be very lonely for you," objected Frank.

"No; I shall have my thoughts for company. When I am alone I can think best of my future plans."

"Won't you come to our house to meals, then?"

"Thank you, Frank! I will do that."

"When is the auction to be?"

"To-day is Monday. It is appointed for Thursday."

"I hope there will be something left for you."

"There will be about enough left to pay my father's small debts and his funeral expenses. I would not like to have him indebted to others for those. I don't think there will be anything over."

Frank looked perplexed.

"I am sorry for you, Phil," he said. "I wish we were rich, instead of having hard work to make both ends meet. You would not lack for anything then."

"Dear Frank," said Philip earnestly, "I never doubted your true friendship. But I am not afraid that I shall suffer. I am sure I can earn my living."

"But why do you shut yourself up alone, Philip?" asked Frank, not satisfied to leave his friend in what he considered the gloomy solitude of a house just visited by death.

"I want to look over my father's papers. I may find out something that I ought to know, and after the auction it will be too late. Father had some directions to give me, but he did not live long enough to do it. For three days I have the house to myself. After that I shall perhaps never visit it again."

"Don't be downhearted, Philip," said Frank, pressing his hand with boyish sympathy.

"I don't mean to be, Frank. I am naturally cheerful and hopeful. I shall miss my poor father sadly: but grieving will not bring him back. I must work for my living, and as I have no money to depend upon, I cannot afford to lose any time in forming my plans."

"You will come over to our house and take your meals!"

"Yes, Frank."

Frank Dunbar's father was a small farmer, who, as Frank had said, found it hard work to make both ends meet. Among all the village boys, he was the one whom Philip liked best, though there were many others whose fathers were in hotter circumstances. For this, however, Philip cared little. Rich or poor, Frank suited him, and they had always been known as chums, to adopt the term used by the boys in the village.

It may be thought that as Philip's circumstances were no better, such an intimacy was natural enough. But Philip Gray possessed special gifts, which made his company sought after. He was a fine singer, and played with considerable skill on the violin - an accomplishment derived from his father, who had acted as his teacher. Then he was of a cheerful temperament, and this is a gift which usually renders the possessor popular, unless marred by positive defects or bad qualities. There were two or three young snobs in the village who looked down upon Philip on account of his father's poverty, but most were very glad to associate with our hero, and have him visit their homes. He was courteous to all, but made - no secret of his preference for Frank Dunbar.

When Philip parted from Frank, and entered the humble dwelling which had been his own and his father's home for years, there was a sense of loneliness and desolation which came over him at first.

His father was the only relative whom he knew, and his death, therefore, left the boy peculiarly, alone in the world. Everything reminded him of his dead father. But he did not allow himself to dwell upon thoughts that would depress his spirits and unfit him for the work that lay before him.

He opened his father's desk and began to examine his papers. There was no will, for there was nothing to leave, but in one compartment of the desk was a thick wallet, which he opened.

In it, among some receipted bills, was an envelope, on which was written, in his father's well-known hand:

"The contents of this envelope are probably of no value, but it will be as well to preserve the certificate of stock. There is a bare possibility that it may some day be worth a trifle."

Philip opened the envelope and found a certificate for a hundred shares of the Excelsior Gold Mine, which appeared to be located in California. He had once heard his father speak of it in much the same terms as above.

"I may as well keep it," reflected Philip. "It will probably amount to nothing, but there won't be much trouble in carrying around the envelope." He also found a note of hand for a thousand dollars, signed by Thomas Graham.

Attached to it was a slip of paper, on which he read, also in his father's writing:

"This note represents a sum of money lent to Thomas

Graham, when I was moderately prosperous. It is now outlawed, and payment could not be enforced, even if Graham were alive and possessed the ability to pay. Five years since, he left this part of the country for some foreign country, and is probably dead, and I have heard nothing from him in all that time. It will do no harm, and probably no good, to keep his note,"

"I will keep it," decided Philip. "It seems that this and the mining shares are all that father had to leave me. They will probably never yield me a cent, but I will keep them in remembrance of him."

Phillip found his father's watch. It was an old-fashioned gold watch, but of no great value even when new. Now, after twenty years' use, it would command a very small price at the coming sale.

Ever since Philip had been old enough to notice anything, he remembered this watch, which was so closely identified with his father that more than anything else it called him to mind. Philip looked at it wistfully as it lay in his hand. "I wish I could keep it," he said to himself. "No one else will value it much, but it would always speak to me of my father. I wonder if I might keep it?"

Philip had a mind to put it into his pocket, but the spirit of honesty forbade.

"It must be sold," he said, with a sigh. "Without it there wouldn't be enough to pay what we owe, and when I leave Norton, I don't want any one to say that my father died in his debt."

There was nothing else in the desk which called for

particular notice or appeared to be of any special value. After a careful examination, Philip closed it and looked around at the familiar furniture of the few rooms which the house contained.

There was one object which he personally valued more than anything else. This was his violin, on which he had learned all that he knew of playing. His father had bought it for him four years before. It was not costly, but it was of good tone, and Philip had passed many pleasant hours in practicing on it.

"I can take this violin, at any rate," said Philip to himself. "It belongs to me, and no one else has a claim on it. I think I will take it with me and leave it at Frank Dunbar's, so that it needn't get into the sale."

He put back the violin into the case and laid it on one side. Then he sat down in the arm-chair, which had been his father's favorite seat, and tried to fix his mind upon the unknown future which lay before him.

He had sat there for half an hour, revolving in his mind various thoughts and plans, when he heard a tap on the window, and looking up, saw through the pane the coarse, red face of Nick Holden, a young fellow of eighteen, the son of the village butcher.

"Let me in!" said Nick; "I want to see you on business."

CHAPTER III.

NICK HOLDEN'S CALL.

Philip had never liked Nick Holden. He was a coarse, rough-looking boy, his reddish face one mass of freckles, and about as unattractive as a person could be, without absolute deformity. This, however, was not the ground for Philip's dislike.

With all his unattractiveness, Nick might have possessed qualities which would have rightly made him popular. So far from this, however, he was naturally mean, selfish, and a bully, with very slight regard for truth.

Will it be believed that, in spite of his homely face, Nick really thought himself good-looking and aspired to be a beau? For this reason he had often wished that he possessed Philip's accomplishment of being able to play upon the violin.

His conversational powers were rather limited, and he felt at a loss when he undertook to make himself fascinating to the young ladies in the village. If he could only play on the violin like Philip he thought he would be irresistible.

He had therefore conceived the design of buying

Philip's instrument for a trifle, judging that our hero would feel compelled to sell it.

The reader will now understand the object which led to Nick's call so soon after the funeral of Mr. Gray. He was afraid some one else might forestall him in gaining possession of the coveted instrument.

When Philip saw who his visitor was, he was not overjoyed. It was with reluctance that he rose and gave admission to Nick.

"I thought I would call around and see you, Phil," said Nick, as he sat down in the most comfortable chair in the room.

"Thank you," responded Phil coldly.

"The old man went off mighty sudden," continued Nicholas, with characteristic delicacy.

"Do you mean my father?" inquired Philip.

"Of course I do. There ain't any one else dead, is there!"

"I had been expecting my poor father's death for some time," said Philip gravely.

"Just so! He wa'n't very rugged. We've all got to come to it sooner or later. I expect dad'll die of apoplexy some time-he's so awful fat," remarked Nicholas cheerfully. "If he does, it's lucky he's got me to run the business. I'm only eighteen, but I can get along as well as anybody. I'm kinder smart in business."

"I am glad you are smart in anything," thought Philip; for he knew that Nick was a hopeless dunce in school duties.

"I hope your father'll live a good while," he said politely.

"Yes, of course," said Nick lightly. "I'd be sorry to have the old man pop off; but then you never can tell about such a thing as that."

Philip did not relish the light way in which Nick referred to such a loss as he was suffering from, and, by way of changing the subject, said:

"I believe you said you came on business, Nicholas?"

"Yes; that's what I wanted to come at. It's about your fiddle."

"My violin!" said Philip, rather surprised.

"Oh, well, fiddle or violin! what's the odds? I want to buy it."

"What for?"

"To play on, of course! What did you think I wanted it for?"

"But you can't play, can you?"

"Not yet; but I expect you could show me some - now, couldn't you?"

"What put it into your head to want to play on the

violin?" asked Philip, with some curiosity.

"Why, you see, the girls like it. It would be kind of nice when I go to a party, or marm has company, to scrape off a tune or two-just like you do. It makes a feller kinder pop'lar with the girls, don't you see?" said Nick, with a knowing grin.

"And you want to be popular with the young ladies!" said Philip, smiling, in spite of his bereavement, at the idea being entertained by such a clumsy-looking caliban as Nick Holden.

"Of course I do!" answered Nick, with another grin. "You see I'm gettin' along-I'll be nineteen next month, and I might want to get married by the time I'm twenty-one, especially if the old man should drop off sudden."

"I understand all that, Nicholas -"

"Call me Nick. I ain't stuck up if I am most a man. Call me pet names, dearest."

And Nicholas laughed loudly at his witty quotation.

"Just as you prefer. Nick, then, I understand your object. But what made you think I wanted to sell the violin?"

It was Nick's turn to be surprised.

"Ain't there goin' to be an auction of your father's things?" he said.

"Yes; but the violin is mine, and I am not going to

sell it."

"You'll have to," said Nick.

"What do you mean by that, Nicholas Holden?" said Philip quickly.

"Because you'll have to sell everything to pay your father's debt. My father said so this very morning."

"I think I know my own business best," said Philip coldly. "I shall keep the violin."

"Maybe it ain't for you to say," returned Nick, apparently not aware of his insolence. "Come, now, I'll tell you what I'll do. My father's got a bill against yours for a dollar and sixty-four cents. I told father I had a use for the fiddle, and he says if you'll give it to me, he'll call it square. There, what do you say to that?"

Nicholas leaned back in his chair and looked at Philip through his small, fishy eyes, as if he had made an uncommonly liberal offer. As for Philip, he hardly knew whether to be angry or amused.

"You offer me a dollar and sixty-four cents for my violin?" he repeated.

"Yes. It's second-hand, to be sure, but I guess it's in pretty fair condition. Besides, you might help me a little about learnin' how to play."

"How much do you suppose the violin cost?" inquired Philip.

"Couldn't say."

"It cost my father twenty-five dollars."

"Oh, come, now, that's too thin! You don't expect a feller to believe such a story as that?"

"I expect to be believed, for I never tell anything but the truth."

"Oh, well, I don't expect yon do, generally, but when it comes to tradin', most everybody lies," observed Nick candidly.

"I have no object in misrepresenting, for I don't want to sell the violin."

"You can't afford to keep it! The town won't let you!"

"The town won't let me?" echoed Philip, now thoroughly mystified.

"Of course they won't. The idea of a pauper bein' allowed a fiddle to play on! Why, it's ridiculous!"

"What do you mean?" demanded Philip, who now began to comprehend the meaning of this thick-witted visitor. "What have I got to do with the town, or with paupers?"

"Why, you're goin' to the poorhouse, ain't you?"

"Certainly not!" answered Philip, with flashing eyes.

"I guess you're mistaken," said Nick coolly. "Squire Pope was over to our shop this mornin', and he told dad that the seleckmen were goin' to send you there after the auction."

Horatio Alger

Philip's eyes flashed angrily. He felt insulted and outraged. Never for a moment had he conceived the idea that any one would regard him as a candidate for the poorhouse.

He had an honorable pride in maintaining himself, and would rather get along on one meal a day, earned by himself in honest independence, than be indebted to public charity even for a luxurious support.

"Squire Pope doesn't know what he's talking about," retorted Philip, who had to exercise some self-restraint not to express himself more forcibly "and you can tell him so when you see him. I am no more likely to go to the poorhouse than you are!"

"Come, that's a good one," chuckled Nick. "Talk of me goin' to the poorhouse, when my father pays one of the biggest taxes in town! Of course, it's different with you."

"You'll have to excuse me now," said Philip, determined to get rid of his disagreeable companion. "I have something to do."

"Then you won't sell me the fiddle, Phil?"

"No, I won't," answered our hero, with scant ceremony.

"Then I'll have to bid it off at the auction. Maybe I'll get it cheaper."

And Mr. Nicholas Holden at length relieved Philip of his company.

CHAPTER IV.

THE AUCTION.

It so happened that Nick Holden met Squire Pope on the village street, and, being rather disappointed at the result of his negotiations with Philip, thought it might be a good idea to broach the subject to the squire, who, as he knew, had taken it upon himself to superintend the sale of Mr. Gray's goods."

"I say, squire, I've just been over to see Phil Gray."

"Ahem! Well, how does he seem to feel?"

"Kinder stuck up, I reckon. He said he wouldn't go to the poorhouse, and I might tell you so."

"I apprehend," said the squire, in his stately way, "he will be under the necessity of going, whether he likes it or not."

"Just so; that's what I told him!" interjected Nick.

"And he should be grateful for so comfortable a home," continued the public man.

"Well, I dunno," said Nick. "They do say that old Tucker most starves the paupers. Why his bills with dad are awful small."

"The town cannot afford to pamper the appetites of its beneficiaries," said the squire. "Where is Philip now?"

"I guess he's at home. I offered to buy his fiddle, but he said he was going to keep it. I offered him a dollar and sixty-four cents - the same as dad's bill against his father, but he wouldn't take it."

"Really, Nicholas, your offer was very irregular - extremely irregular. It should have been made to me, as the administrator of the late Mr. Gray, and not to a boy like Philip."

"Will you sell me the fiddle for dad's bill, squire?" asked Nicholas eagerly.

"You are premature, Nicholas -"

"What's that?"

"I mean you must wait till the auction. Then you will have a chance to bid on the instrument, if you want to secure it."

"Phil says it's his, and won't be for sale at the auction."

"Then Philip is mistaken. He is only a boy. The estate will be settled by those who are older and wiser than he."

"I guess you'll find him hard to manage, squire," said Nick, laughing.

"We shall see - we shall see," returned the squire.

And, with a dignified wave of the hand, he cotinued on his walk.

After the visit of Nicholas, Philip thought it most prudent to convey the violin which he prized so much to the house of his friend, Frank Dunbar, where he had been invited to take his meals.

He was willing to have the furniture sold to defray his father's small debts, but the violin was his own. It had not even been given him by his father. Though the latter purchased it, the money which it cost had been given to Philip by a friend of the family. He rightly thought that he had no call to sell it now.

"Frank," said he to his boy-friend, "I want you to put away my violin safely, and keep it until after the auction."

"Of course I will, Phil; but won't you want to play on it!"

"Not at present. I'll tell you why I want it put away."

And Philip told his friend about Nick's application to purchase it, and the liberal offer he had made.

"Nick's generosity never will hurt him much," said Frank, laughing. "What in the world did he want of your violin?"

"He wants to make himself popular with the girls."

"He'll never do that, even if he learns to play like an angel!" said Frank. "You ought to hear the girls talk about him. He couldn't get a single one of them to go home with from singing-school last winter. He teased my sister to go, but she told him every time she was engaged to some one else."

The two days that intervened between the funeral and the auction passed, and the last scene connecting Philip with the little cottage which had been his home was to take place.

In a country town, an auction-however inconsiderable-draws together an interested company of friends and neighbors; and, though no articles of value were to be sold, this was the case at the present sale.

Philip didn't at first mean to be present. He thought it would only give him pain; but at the last moment he came, having been requested to do so by Squire Pope, as information might be required which he could give.

The bulk of the furniture was soon disposed of, at low prices, to be sure, but sufficiently high to make it clear that enough would be realized to pay the small bills outstanding.

Philip's lip quivered when his father's watch was put up. He would have liked to buy it, but this was impossible; for he had only about a dollar of his own.

Nick Holden's eyes sparkled when he saw the watch. He had forgotten about that, but as soon as he saw it he coveted it. He had a cheap silver watch of his own, which he had bought secondhand about three years before. He had thought that he might some day possess a gold watch, but he was not willing to lay out the necessary sum of money.

By dint of actual meanness, he had laid up two hundred dollars, which he now had in the savings-bank in the next village, and he could therefore have bought one if he had chosen; but, like Gilpin, "Though on pleasure bent, he had a frugal mind."

Now, however, there seemed a chance of getting a gold watch at a low price. Nick reasoned rightly that at an auction it would go much below its value, and it would be a good thing for him to buy it-even as an investment-as he would probably have chances enough to trade it off at a handsome profit,

"I shouldn't wonder if I could double my money on it," he reflected.

Accordingly, when the watch was put up, Nick eagerly bid two dollars.

Philip's lip curled when he heard this generous bid, and he heartily hoped that this treasured possession of his dead father might not fall into such hands.

Nick rather hoped that no one would bid against him, but in this he was destined to be disappointed.

"Five dollars!" was next heard.

And this bid came from Mr. Dunbar, the father of his friend Frank. Philip's eyes brightened up, for there was no one he would sooner see the possessor of the watch than his kind friend.

Nick looked chopfallen when he heard this large increase on his original bid, and hesitated to continue, but finally mustered up courage to say, in a rather feeble tone:

"Five and a quarter."

"Five dollars and a quarter bid!" said the auctioneer. "Do I hear more?"

"Six dollars," said Mr. Dunbar quietly.

The bid was repeated, and the auctioneer waited for a higher one, but Nick retired ignominiously from the contest.

He wasn't sure whether he could get much over six dollars for it himself, and he foresaw that Mr. Dunbar intended to have it, even if it cost considerable more.

"It's kinder hard on a feller," he complained to the man standing next him. "What does Mr. Dunbar want of the watch? He's got one already,"

"Perhaps he thinks it is a good bargain at the price."

"It's what I've been wantin' all along," said Nick. "He might have let me have it."

"Why don't you bid more?"

"I wanted to get it cheap."

"And the auctioneer wants to get as much as he can for the articles, and so do Philip's friends," This was a consideration which, of course, had no weight with Nicholas. However, he had one comfort. He would bid on the violin, and probably no one else would bid against it. He did not see it, to be sure, but concluded, of course, that it would be bid off. When the sale drew near the end, he went to Philip, and said:

"Whereabouts is the fiddle, Phil?"

"It isn't here," answered our hero.

"Ain't it goin' to be sold?"

"Of course not! It's mine. I told you that once already."

"We'll see!" said Nicholas angrily.

And going up to Squire Pope, he held a brief conversation with that gentleman.

The squire nodded vigorously, and walked over to Philip.

"Philip," said he, "go and bring your violin."

"What will I do that for!" asked our hero quietly.

"So that it may be sold."

"It is not to be sold," returned Philip quietly. "It belongs to me."

"Nothing belongs to you except your clothes!" said the squire angrily. "I require you to go and fetch the instrument."

"And I decline to do it," said Philip.

"Do you know who I am," demanded the squire, with ruffled dignity.

"I know you perfectly well," answered Philip "but I am the owner of the violin, and I don't mean to have it sold."

"YOU will repent this!" said Squire Pope, who felt that his lawful authority and official dignity were set at naught.

Philip bowed and left the house. He did not know what steps the squire might take, but he was resolved not to give up his cherished violin.

CHAPTER V.

AN ALLIANCE AGAINST PHILIP.

Squire Pope was not a bad man, nor was he by nature a tyrant, but he was so fully convinced of his own superior judgment that he was in all things obstinately bent on having his own way. He had persuaded himself that our young hero, Philip, would be better off in the poorhouse than in a place where he could earn his own living, and no one could convince him to the contrary.

As to the boy's feelings on the subject, he considered those of no importance. He had good reason to know that Philip would object to being an inmate of the almshouse, but he was determined that he should go there.

In like manner, before the auction was over, he saw clearly that it would realize a sum more than sufficient to pay the funeral expenses of the late Mr. Gray and the few small bills outstanding against his estate, and that there was no necessity that Philip's violin should be sold, but none the less he resolved that it should be sold.

"Shall I allow a young lad to dictate to me?" Squire Pope asked himself, in irritation. "Certainly not! I know better what is right than he. It is ridiculous that a town pauper should own a violin. Why, the next thing, we shall have to buy pianos for our almshouses, for the use of the gentlemen and ladies who occupy them. A violin, indeed!"

This Squire Pope regarded as irresistible logic and withering sarcasm combined.

He saw Philip go out of the cottage, but, as the sale was not over, he was unable to follow him.

"Never mind, I'll fix him as soon as I have time," he said to himself.

"Back so soon? Is the auction over!" asked his friend, Frank Dunbar, who was engaged in splitting wood in the rear of the house.

"No, Frank, not quite; but it's almost over..Who do you think bid on father's gold watch?"

"I don't know."

"Nick Holden."

"He didn't get it, did he?"

"I am glad to say not. Your father bought it."

"Did he! Why, he's got one watch already."

"I am glad he's got it. I couldn't bear to think of Nick Holden carrying my father's watch. He was disappointed about one thing besides."

"What was that?"

"The violin. He went to Squire Pope, and complained that it was not in the sale."

"That's just like his impudence. What did the squire say?"

"He came to me and ordered me to get it, so that it might be sold."

"Shall I get it for you, then?"

"Not much!" answered Philip emphatically. "It is mine, as I have already told you. If the auction doesn't bring in enough to settle up everything, I may agree to sell it for a fair price; but I am sure, from the prices, that it won't be necessary."

"Squire Pope's a dreadful obstinate man," said Frank doubtfully. "He may insist upon your selling the violin."

"Let him do it!" said Philip contemptuously. "I should like to see him get it. Where have you put it, Frank?"

"Where Squire Pope won't be apt to find it - in an old chest up in the garret. It's full of old clothes, belonging to my grandfather, and hasn't been looked into by any one except me for years. I put it away under all the clothes at the bottom. No one knows where it is except you and me, not even mother."

"That's good. I guess we can defy the squire, then."

Half an hour later, Mr. Dunbar came home from the auction.

Philip went to meet him.

"Thank you for buying father's watch," he said. "But for you, Nick Holden would have had it, and I should have been sorry for it."

"He was badly disappointed," said Mr. Dunbar smiling. "But I didn't buy the watch for myself, Philip."

"For whom, then?" asked Philip, in some surprise.

"For the one that has the best right to it - for you," and the farmer took the watch from his pocket, and handed it to Philip.

"But I haven't the money to pay for it, Mr. Dunbar," said our hero.

"Then I give it to you as a present," said Mr. Dunbar.

"I am very grateful," said Philip; "but I ought not to accept it. You are too kind to me."

"Let me be the judge of that."

"Besides, it wouldn't be safe for me to take it. Squire Pope will try to get my violin away from me in order to sell it, and he would be sure to try to do the same by the watch if he found that I had it."

"But, Philip, I don't need the watch myself."

"Then, Mr. Dunbar, will you be kind enough to keep it for me, and when I can afford to pay for it, and there is no danger of its being taken from me, I will ask you for it. I shall be very glad, indeed, when I am older, to carry my father's watch, for I have seen it in his hands so often that it will constantly remind me of him."

"Perhaps that will be the best arrangement," said Mr. Dunbar. "You might have it stolen from you, if you carried it yourself just at present. As you request, I will keep it, subject to your order; but I would rather let it be a gift from me, and not require you to pay for it."

"We won't talk about that now," said Philip, smiling. "At any rate, you must let me thank you for your great kindness to me."

"Don't speak of that, Phil," said the farmer kindly. "I had a great respect and liking for your father, and I verily believe my Frank loves you as well as if you were his own brother. So, come what may, you have a friend in our family."

"I indorse all that father says," Frank said.

And he extended his hand to Philip, who grasped it heartily.

It warmed his heart to think that he had such good friends, though he was an orphan and alone in the world.

After supper, Mr. Dunbar went to the village store, while Frank and Philip remained at home.

Suddenly Frank said:

"Philip, you are going to have a visitor, I guess."

"A visitor!"

"Yes; I saw Squire Pope stumping along the road, nourishing his gold-headed cane. He is headed this way, and it's likely he is going to honor you with a call. He's got somebody with him, too. Who is it!"

Philip shaded his eyes with his hand, for the Sun was near its setting, and shining with dazzling brightness from the quarter toward which he was looking.

"It's Nick Holden!" he said.

"So it is! What can he want?"

"I understand very well. He wants my violin. He couldn't get it at the sale, so he has come here to see if he can't make me give it to him."

"And will you?"

"You ought to know me better than to ask, Frank," said Philip firmly. "Nick might as well have stayed away, for he won't accomplish anything."

Nick, however, held a different opinion. After Philip left the cottage, he had gone to Squire Pope, and cunningly asked:

"Are you going to let Philip keep his fiddle in spite of you, squire?"

"What do you mean, Nicholas?" demanded the squire, in a stately way.

"Why, seems to me he's kinder settin' up his will agin

yours. You say the fiddle shall be sold, and he says it shan't. He told me he didn't care what you said, he should keep it."

"Did he say that, Nicholas?" asked the squire, who felt that his dignity was outraged by such insolence.

"I'm sartain he did. He's pretty big feelin', Phil is. He always wants to have his own way."

"He will find that he can't defy me with impunity," said the squire stiffly.

"Just so. Then you'll sell me the fiddle?"

"I will!" said the squire emphatically.

"You won't ask too much, will you?" asked Nick anxiously.

Now Squire Pope, who knew nothing of the price of violins, and had a very inadequate idea of their value, after some haggling on the part of Nick, agreed to sell him the instrument for two dollars and a half, and to see that it was delivered that evening.

"Do you know where it is, Nicholas?" he asked.

"Why, Phil is staying over at Frank Dunbar's, and I guess he's got it there somewhere. I guess we'd better go over there and get it."

"Very well, Nicholas. After supper, if you will come to my house, I will go over there, and see that you have the instrument."

"All right, squire!" said Nick gleefully, "Phil will find that he can't have his own way this time."

"I apprehend he will," said the squire complacently.

Now the reader understands how it happened that Squire Pope and Nick Holden made a call on Philip. As to what passed at the interview, we must refer him to the next chapter.

CHAPTER VI.

FUSS ABOUT A FIDDLE.

"Ahem! Good evening!" said Squire Pope to Frank Dunbar, taking no notice of Philip's cold but polite salutation.

"Good evening! Will you go into the house?" said Frank.

"I believe not. I have not time."

"I am sorry father isn't home. He just started for the village."

"Ahem! it was not to see your father that I called," answered Squire Pope. "I wish to have a few words with this young man," indicating Philip stiffly.

"I am at your service, Squire Pope," said Philip, with ceremonious politeness.

"We came about the fiddle," interrupted Nick Holden, who always wanted to have a share in the conversation.

Squire Pope frowned, for he did not relish Nick's interference.

"Nicholas," he said severely, "I apprehend I am competent to manage the business we have come upon."

"Don't get riled, squire," said Nick, by no means abashed by this rebuke. "I thought you were kinder slow about comin' to the point."

"Your interruption was very indecorous. I do not require any assistance or any suggestions."

"All right, squire!"

Squire Pope now turned to our hero, and said:

"As I was about to say, when interrupted by Nicholas, I have come to require you to give up - the Violin which, without authority and against my express command, you withheld from the auction."

"The violin is mine, Squire Pope," said Philip firmly, "and I mean to keep it!"

"You talk like an ignorant boy. As a minor, you had no claim to the possession of any article except your clothing. I judged it best that the violin should be sold at the auction, and it is presumptuous for you to set up your judgment against mine!"

"I don't take that view of it," said Philip, and then he stopped.

He knew it was of no use to argue against the squire, who was obstinate to the verge of pig-headedness, if I may be allowed to use the expression. He felt that it would be only wasting his breath.

"It is quite immaterial how you view the subject," said the squire pompously. "My mind is made up, and my resolution is not likely to be shaken by a boy."

"Then, sir," answered Philip, in a respectful tone but with a slight smile, "it is hardly worth while for me to say any more."

"I am glad you have arrived at so sensible a conclusion," said Squire Pope. "I take it that you have the violin here."

"Yes, sir."

"Then bring it out and give it to me."

Now came the critical point, when Philip must array himself in determined opposition to Squire Pope. He felt that he was entirely in the right; still he regretted the necessity of the antagonism.

Philip had one thing in his favor: He had plenty of self-control, and, although he was very indignant at the course of the squire, which he regarded as unjusti-fiable, he made up his mind to be as respectful as circumstances would permit.

"I don't think you understand me, Squire Pope," he said. "I refuse to give up the violin!"

"You refuse to give up the violin!" repeated Squire Pope, scarcely believing the testimony of his ears. "Do I hear you aright?"

"Yes, sir."

Horatio Alger

"I never see such impudence!" ejaculated Nick Holden, wishing to egg on the squire.

"Do you mean to defy me to my face?" demoded Squire Pope, growing very red.

"I don't wish to defy you or anybody else," returned Philip; "but I shall stand up for my rights."

"Misguided boy!" said the squire severely; "you will yet rue this rash and heedless course. Frank," he continued, turning to Frank Dunbar, "do you know where Philip's violin is!"

"Yes, sir."

"Do me the favor to bring it out and place it in my hands."

"You must excuse me, Squire Pope," answered Frank. "It belongs to Philip, and I have no right to meddle with it."

"If Philip has told you this, he has misrepresented," said the squire, rather discouraged by this second rebuff. "The violin does not belong to Philip. It belongs to this young man."

And, with a wave of his hand, he designated Nick Holden.

It was not polite, but Frank Dunbar was so surprised by this announcement that he whistled.

As for Philip, he regarded Nick calmly; but there didn't seem to be any sign of yielding in his look.

"It belongs to Nicholas, because I have sold it to him," continued Squire Pope doggedly.

"That's so!" corroborated Nick complacently. "The squire sold me the fiddle for two-fifty. It's mine now, and you'd better fetch it along out, or there'll be trouble."

Philip turned to Squire Pope, and said quietly:

"As you had no right to sell it, the sale amounts to nothing. If you had a right, I should say you were not very shrewd to sell an instrument that cost twenty-five dollars - and was considered a bargain at the price - for two dollars and fifty cents."

"The violin cost twenty-five dollars!" ejaculated the squire, in genuine surprise.

For, as it has already been stated, he had no idea whatever of the usual price for a violin.

"Yes, sir."

"Don't you believe him, squire," said Nicholas, afraid that he would lose what he knew to be a good bargain. "No fiddle that was ever made cost twenty-five dollars. It's ridiculous!"

"It does seem a large price," said the squire guardedly.

Squire Pope would doubtless have been surprised to learn that certain violins of celebrated make - such as the Cremonas - have sold for thousands of dollars. Probably he would have disbelieved it.

Nevertheless, he began to think that he had been too precipitate in accepting Nick Holden's offer.

If he should sacrifice, or sell at an utterly inadequate price, any article belonging to the boy whom he considered his ward, he knew that he would be blamed, and he began to consider how he could recede from the bargain.

"Nicholas," he said, "I didn't exactly sell the violin to yon. I will ascertain what is a fair price for it, and then I will consider your proposal."

"You sold it right out, squire," said Nick, "and I can prove it. Didn't you just say it was mine. There, now!"

Nick turned triumphantly to Frank and Phil, but, for very good reasons, they did not care to side with him.

"I say, you haven't treated me right," persisted Nick, who had no particular respect nor veneration for the squire, and was not to be deterred from speaking as he felt. "I offered you two-fifty, and you said I should have it, and you got me to call at your house to come here for it."

"I cannot sacrifice the property of my ward," said Squire Pope. "I must ascertain how much the violin is worth."

"A bargain is a bargain, every time!" said Nick, irritated.

"I will let you have it as cheap as anybody," said the squire, who thought it possible that Nick might be the only one who desired to purchase it. "That ought to satisfy you. Philip, go and bring me the violin, and I will carry it home and dispose of it to the best advantage."

"You must excuse me, Squire Pope. I shall not let it leave my possession." Just then Squire Pope espied Mr. Dunbar returning from the village, and hailed him as a probable ally. He laid the matter before him, and requested him to compel Philip to get the violin.

"You must excuse me, squire," said Mr. Dunbar coldly. "Philip is my guest, and he shall be protected in his rights as long as he remains here."

Without a word, Squire Pope walked off, in angry discomfiture, in one direction, while Nick, equally dissatisfied, walked off in another.

"They don't seem happy!" said Frank slyly.

"I wish I knew where it was going to end," returned Philip gravely.

"It seems to me," said Frank, "the squire is making a great fuss about a fiddle, for a man of his dignity."

"He doesn't care about the violin. He wants to have his own way," said Philip, thus hitting the nail on the head.

CHAPTER VII.

MR. JOE TUCKER

Before going further, I will introduce to the reader, a citizen of Norton, who filled a position for which he was utterly unfitted. This man was Joe Tucker, in charge of the almshouse.

He had not been selected by the town authorities on the ground of fitness, but simply because he was willing to work cheap. He received a certain low weekly sum for each one of his inmates, and the free use of apartments for himself and family, with the right to cultivate the ten acres of land connected with the establishment, and known as the Town Farm.

His family consisted of three persons - himself, his wife, and a son, Ezekiel, familiarly known as Zeke, now sixteen years old. The leading family trait was meanness.

Mr. Tucker supplied a mean table even for a poorhouse, and some of the hapless inmates comp-lained bitterly. One had even had the boldness to present a complaint to the selectmen, and that body, rather reluctantly, undertook to investigate the justness of the complaint. They deputed Squire Pope to visit the poorhouse and inquire into the matter.

Now, though Squire Pope thought himself unusually sharp, it was the easiest thing in the world for a cunning person like Joe Tucker to satisfy him that all was right.

"Mr. Tucker," said Squire Pope pompously, "I am deputed by the selectmen, and I may add by the overseers of the poor, to investigate a complaint made by one of the paupers in relation to the fare you offer them."

"Who is it!" inquired Mr. Tucker.

"It is Ann Carter. She says you don't allow her sugar in her tea, and only allow one slice of bread at supper, and that the meat is so bad she can't eat it."

"Just like the old woman!" exclaimed Mr. Tucker indignantly. "Oh, she's a high-strung pauper, she is! Expects all the delicacies of the season for seventy-five cents a week. She'd ought to go to the Fifth Avenoo Hotel in New York, and then I'll bet a cent she wouldn't be satisfied."

It is observable that even in his imaginary bets Mr. Tucker maintained his economical habits, and seldom bet more than a cent. Once, when very much excited, he had bet five cents, but this must be attributed to his excited state of mind.

"So you regard her complaints as unreasonable, do you, Mr. Tucker?" observed the investigating committee.

"Unreasonable? I should think they was. I allow, Squire Pope, we don't live like a first-class hotel" - Mr.

Tucker's language was rather mixed - "but we live as well as we can afford to. As to sugar, we don't allow the paupers to put it in for themselves, or they'd ruin us by their extravagance. Mrs. Tucker puts sugar in the teapot before she pours it out. I s'pose Ann Carter would put as much in one cup of tea as Mrs. T. uses for the whole teapotful, if she had her way."

This was very probably true, as the frugal Mrs. Tucker only allowed one teaspoonful for the entire supply.

"That looks reasonable, Mr. Tucker," said the squire approvingly. "Now about the bread and the meat?"

"The paupers has plenty of bread," said Mr. Tucker. "Our bread bill is actually enormous."

"And as to the meat?"

"We don't give 'em roast turkey every day, and we don't buy tenderloin steaks to pamper their appetites," said Mr. Tucker, "though we're perfectly willing to do it if the town'll pay us so we can afford it. Do you think the town'll agree to pay me twenty-five cents more a week for each one, squire?"

"Certainly not. It can't be thought of," said the squire hastily, knowing that if the selectmen advocated such a measure they would probably lose their reelection.

"If it would, we might live a little better, so that Ann Carter wouldn't have to complain, though, bless your soul! that woman is always complainin'."

"Ahem! Mr. Tucker, you present the matter to me in a new light. I really feel that Ann Carter is very unreasonable in her complaints."

"I knowed you'd do me justice, squire," said Mr. Tucker effusively. "You're a sharp man. You ain't a-goin' to be taken in by any of them paupers' rigmarole. I always said, Squire Pope, that you was the right man in the right place, and that the town was lucky to have so intelligent and public-spirited a citizen fillin' her most important offices."

"Mr. Tucker," said the squire, "you gratify me. It has ever been my aim to discharge with conscientious fidelity the important trusts which the town has committed to my charge -"

"I'll bear witness to that, squire."

"And your sincere tribute gives me great satisfaction."

"I hope you'll report things right to the board, Squire Pope?" said Mr. Job Tucker insinuatingly.

"Be assured I will, Mr. Tucker. I consider you a zealous and trustworthy official, striving hard to do your duty in the place the town has assigned you."

"I do, indeed, squire," said Mr. Tucker, pulling on a red handkerchief and mopping some imaginary tears. "Excuse my emotions, sir, but your generous confidence quite unmans me. I - I - trust now that I shall be able to bear meekly the sneers and complaints of Ann Carter and her fellow paupers."

"I will stand by you, Mr. Tucker," said Squire Pope cordially, for the man's flattery, coarse as it was, had been like incense to his vanity. "I will stand by you, and uphold you by my testimony."

"Thank you, squire. With such an impartial advocate I will continue to do my duty and fear nothing."

As Squire Pope left the almshouse, Mr. Tucker winked at himself in the glass, and said quizzically:

"I guess I'm all right now. The vain old fool thinks he's a second Solomon, and thinks I regard him as such. Oh, it takes me to get round him!"

Squire Pope wrote an elaborate report, in which he stated that, after searching investigation, he had ascertained that the complaints of Ann Carter were absolutely groundless, and gave it as his conviction that Mr. Tucker's treatment of her and her associate paupers was characterized by remarkable consideration and humanity.

Such officials as he have much to answer for, and yet there are plenty just as false to their responsibilities as he.

It was two days after Squire Pope's ineffectual attempt to possess himself of Philip's violin, that our hero was walking along a country road, on his return from an errand which, he had undertaken for his friend's father, when his attention was drawn to the yelping of a small dog, that seemed in fear or pain.

Looking over the stone wall, Philip saw Zeke Tucker amusing himself by thrusting the dog's head into a pool of dirty water, and holding it there till the animal was nearly strangled. The dog's suffering appeared to yield the most exquisite amusement to the boy, who burst into peal after peal of rude laughter as he watched the struggles of his victim.

Philip, like every decent boy, had a horror of cruelty, and the sight stirred him to immediate anger and disgust.

"What are you doing there, Zeke Tucker?" he demanded sternly.

"None of your business!" answered Zeke, frowning.

"You'd better answer my question," said Philip, who had by this time jumped over the wall.

"Then I will. I'm havin' a little fun. What have you got to say about it?" retorted Zeke.

And once more he plunged the head of the poor dog into the filthy pool.

The next moment he found himself floundering on his back, while the dog, slipping from his grasp, was running across the meadows. "What did you do that for!" demanded Zeke, springing up, his face flaming with rage.

"I rather think you understand well enough," answered Philip contemptuously.

"What business have you to touch me? I can have you arrested, you low pauper!"

"What's that? What did you call me?" demanded Philip.

"I called you a pauper."

"By what right?"

"Squire Pope told my father he was going to bring you over to the poorhouse to live. You just see if my father doesn't give it to you then!"

"Thank you," said Phil contemptuously; "but I don't propose to board at your establishment, not even to obtain the pleasure of your society."

"Maybe you can't help yourself," said Zeke gleefully.

For he saw what had escaped the notice of Philip, whose back was turned - namely, a four-seated carryall, containing his father and Squire Pope, which had just halted in the road, hard by.

"Mr. Tucker," said Squire Pope, in a low tone, "now will be the best opportunity to capture the boy and carry him to the almshouse."

"All right - I'm ready" said Tucker readily.

For another boarder would bring him sixty cents a week more.

They stopped the horses and prepared for business.

CHAPTER XIII.

IN THE ENEMY'S HANDS

Philip heard a step, and turned to see whose it was; but, when he recognized Mr. Tucker, the latter's hand was already on his collar.

"What have you been doin' to Zeke? Tell me that, you young rascal" said Mr. Tucker roughly.

"He pitched into me savage, father," answered Zeke, who had picked himself up, and was now engaged in brushing the dust from his coat.

"Pitched into ye, did he?" repeated Joe Tucker grimly. "I reckon he didn't know your father was 'round. What have you got to say for yourself, eh?"

Philip regarded his captor contemptuously, and didn't struggle to escape, knowing that he was not a match for a man five inches taller than himself. But contempt he could not help showing, for he knew very well that Zeke had inherited his mean traits largely from his father.

"I'll thank you to remove your hand from my collar, sir," said Philip. "When you have done that, I will explain why I pitched into Zeke, as he calls it."

"Don't you let go, father!" said Zeke hastily. "He'll run away, if you do."

"If I do, you can catch me between you," returned Philip coolly.

"I reckon that's so," said Mr. Tucker, withdrawing his hand, but keeping wary watch of our hero.

"Now go ahead!" said he.

Philip did so.

"I saw Zeke torturing a small dog," he explained, "and I couldn't stand by and let it go on."

"What was he doin' to him?" inquired Mr. Tucker.

"Putting the poor animal's head into this dirty pool, and keeping it there till it was nearly suffocated."

"Was you doin' that, Zeke?" asked his father.

"I was havin' a little fun with him," said Zeke candidly.

"It might have been fun to you, but it wasn't to him," said Phil.

"Why didn't you ask Zeke to stop, and not fly at him like a tiger?" demanded Mr. Tucker.

"I did remonstrate with him, but he only laughed, and did it again."

"He hadn't no right to order me," said Zeke. "It wa'n't no business of his if I was havin' a little fun with the dog."

"And I had a little fun with, you," returned Philip - "You couldn't have complained if I had dipped your head in the water also."

"I ain't a dog!" said Zeke.

"I should respect you more if you were," said Philip.

"Are you goin' to let him talk to me like that!" asked Zeke, appealing to his father.

"No, I ain't," said Mr. Tucker angrily. "You've committed an assault and battery on my son, you rascal, and you'll find there ain't no fun in it for you. I could have you arrested and put in jail, couldn't I, squire?"

"Ahem! Well, you could have him fined; but, as he is to be under your care, Mr. Tucker, you will have a chance of making him conduct himself properly."

"What do you mean by that, Squire Pope?" asked Philip quickly.

"Young man, I do not choose to be catechized," said Squire Pope, in a dignified manner; "but I have no objections to tell you that I have made arrangements with Mr. Tucker to take you into the poorhouse."

"I've heard that before, but I couldn't believe it", said Philip proudly.

"I guess you'll have to believe it pretty soon. he, he!" laughed Zeke, with a grin which indicated his high delight. "I guess dad'll make you stand round when he gits you into the poor-house."

"Don't you consider me capable of earning my own living, Squire Pope?" asked Philip.

"Ahem! Yes, you will be one of these days. You won't have to stay in the almshouse all your life."

"You'll have a chance to earn your livin' with me." said Mr. Tucker. "I shall give you something to do, you may depend."

"You can make him saw and split wood, father, and do the chores and milk the cow," suggested Zeke.

"I have no objection to doing any of those things for a farmer," said Philip, "but I am not willing to do it where I shall be considered a pauper."

"Kinder uppish!" suggested Mr. Tucker, turning to Squire Pope. "Most all of them paupers is proud; but it's pride in the wrong place, I reckon."

"If it is pride to want to earn an independent living, and not live on charity, then I am proud," continued Philip.

"Well, squire, how is it to be," asked Mr. Tucker.

"Philip," said Squire Pope pompously, "you are very young, and you don't know what is best for you. We do, and you must submit. Mr. Tucker, take him and put him in the wagon, and we'll drive over to the poorhouse."

"What! now?" asked Philip, in dismay.

"Just so," answered Joe Tucker. "When you've got your bird, don't let him go, that's what I say."

"That's the talk, dad!" said Zeke gladfully. "We'll take down his pride, I guess, when we've got him home."

Joe Tucker approached Philip, and was about to lay hold of him, when our hero started back.

"You needn't lay hold of me, Mr. Tucker," he said. "I will get into the wagon if Squire Pope insists upon it."

"I'm glad you're gettin' sensible," said the squire, congratulating himself on finding Philip more tractable than he expected.

"And you will go to the poorhouse peaceful, and without making a fuss?" asked Joe.

"Yes, I will go there; but I won't stay there."

"You won't stay there!" ejaculated the squire.

"No, sir! In treating me as a dependent on charity, you are doing what neither you nor any other man has a right to do," said Philip firmly.

"You don't appear to remember that I am a selectman and overseer of the poor," said the Squire.

"I am aware that you hold those offices; but if so, you ought to save money to the town, and not compel them to pay for my support, when I am willing and able to support myself."

Squire Pope looked a little puzzled. This was putting

the matter in a new light, and he could not help admitting to himself that Philip was correct, and that perhaps his fellow citizens might take the same view.

On the other hand, the squire was fond of having his own way, and he had now gone so far that he could not recede without loss of dignity.

"I think," he answered stiffly, "that I understand my duty as well as a boy of fifteen. I don't mean to keep you here long, but it is the best arrangement for the present."

"Of course it is," said Zeke, well pleased with the humiliation of his enemy.

"Shut up, Zeke!" said his father, observing from the squire's expression that he did not fancy Zeke's interference.

"All right, dad," said Zeke good-naturedly, seeing that things had turned out as he desired.

"Jump in!" said Mr. Tucker to Philip.

Our hero, without a word, obeyed. He was firmly resolved that Squire Pope should not have his way, but he did not choose to make himself ridiculous by an ineffectual resistance which would only have ended in his discomfiture.

Seated between Mr. Tucker and the squire, he was driven rapidly toward the poorhouse.

CHAPTER IX.

THE POORHOUSE.

There was no room for Zeke to ride - that is, there was no seat for him - but he managed to clamber into the back part of the wagon, where he sat, or squatted, rather uncomfortably, but evidently in the best of spirits - if any inference could be drawn from his expression.

The poorhouse was not far away. It was a three-story frame house, which badly needed painting, with a dilapidated barn, and shed near by.

A three-story farmhouse is not common in the country, but this dwelling had been erected by a Mr. Parmenter, in the expectation of making a fortune by taking summer boarders.

There was room enough for them, but they did not come. The situation was the reverse of pleasant, the soil about was barren, and there were no shade or fruit trees. It was a crazy idea, selecting such a spot for a summer boarding-house, and failure naturally resulted.

There had, indeed, been two boarders - a man and his wife - who paid one week's board, and managed to owe six before the unlucky landlord decided that they were a pair of swindlers. He had spent more money than he could afford on his house, and went steadily behind-hand year after year, till the town - which was in want of a poorhouse - stepped in and purchased the house and farm at a bargain. So it came to be a boarding-house, after all, but in a sense not contemplated by the proprietor, and, at present, accommodated eleven persons - mostly old and infirm - whom hard fortune compelled to subsist on charity.

Mr. Tucker had this advantage, that his boarders, had no recourse except to stay with him, however poor his fare or harsh his treatment, unless they were in a position to take care of themselves.

When Philip came in sight of the almshouse - which he had often seen, and always considered a very dreary-looking building - he was strengthened in his determination not long to remain a tenant.

Mr. Tucker drove up to the front door with a flourish.

A hard-featured woman came out, and regarded the contents of the wagon with curiosity.

"Well, Abigail, can you take another boarder!" asked Mr. Tucker, as he descended from the wagon.

"Who is it?"

"Well, it ain't likely to be Squire Pope!" said Joe facetiously; "and Zeke and I are regular boarders on the free list."

"Is it that boy?"

"Yes; it's Phil Gray."

"Humph! boys are a trial!" remarked Mrs. Tucker, whose experience with Zeke had doubtless convinced her of this fact.

"I sha'n't trouble you long, Mrs. Tucker," said Philip. "I don't intend to stay."

"You don't, hey?" retorted Joe Tucker, with a wolfish grin and an emphatic nod of the head. "We'll see about that - won't we, Squire Pope?"

"The boy is rather rebellious, Mrs. Tucker," said the selectman. "He appears to think he knows better what is good for him than we do. You may look upon him as a permanent boarder. What he says is of no account."

Philip said nothing, but he looked full at the squire with an unflinching gaze. If ever determination was written upon any face, it was on his.

"Come down there!" said Mrs. Tucker, addressing our hero. "You're at home now."

"Mr. Dunbar won't know what has become of me," said Philip, with a sudden thought. "They will be anxious. May I go back there and tell them where I am?"

"Do you think I am green enough for that?" Mr. Tucker, touching the side of his nose waggishly. "We shouldn't be likely to set eyes on you again."

"I will promise to come back here this evening," said Philip.

"And will you promise to stay?" asked Squire Pope doubtfully.

"No, sir," answered Philip boldly. "I won't do that, but I will engage to come back. Then Mr. Tucker will have to look out for me, for I tell you and him frankly I don't mean to stay."

"Did you ever hear such talk, squire!" asked Mr. Tucker, with a gasp of incredulity. "He actually defies you, who are a selectman and an overseer of the poor."

"So he does, Mr. Tucker. I'm shocked at his conduct."

"Shall we let him go?"

"No, of course not."

"I agree with you, squire. I know'd you wouldn't agree to it. What shall I do about his wantin' to run away?"

"It will be best to confine him just at first, Mr. Tucker."

"I'll shut him up in one of the attic rooms," said Mr. Tucker.

"I think it will be the best thing to do, Mr. Tucker."

Philip took all this very coolly. As to the way in which they proposed to dispose of him for the present he cared very little, as he did not intend stay till morning if there was any possible chance of getting away. The only thing that troubled him was the doubt and anxiety of his good friends, the Dunbars, when he did not return to the house.

"Squire Pope," he said, turning to that official, "will you do me a favor?"

"Ahem! Explain yourself," said the squire suspiciously.

"Will you call at Mr. Dunbar's and tell them where I am."

Now, for obvious reasons, the squire did not like to do this. He knew that the Dunbars would manifest great indignation at the arbitrary step which he had adopted, and he did not like to face their displeasure, especially as his apology would perforce be a lame one.

"I don't think I am called upon to do you a favor, seeing how you've acted, Philip," he said hesitatingly. "Besides, it would be out of my way, and I ought to get home as soon as possible."

"Then you refuse, sir?"

"Well, I'd rather not."

"Will you get word to them, Mr. Tucker?" asked Philip, turning to him.

"I hain't got time," answered Mr. Tucker, who feared that the Dunbars would come for Philip and release him in the course of the evening.

Philip was nonplused. Always considerate of the feelings of others, he was unwilling that his friends should suffer anxiety on his account.

As Mr. Tucker and Squire Pope walked away together,

our hero turned to Zeke.

"I suppose it's no use to ask you to do me a favor, Zeke?" he said.

"Do you want me to tell Frank Dunbar where you are?"

"Yes, I wish you would."

"Then I'll do it."

"You're a better fellow than I thought you were, Zeke," said Philip, surprised.

"No, I ain't! Do you want to know why I'm willin' to go?"

"Why?"

"I know Frank Dunbar'll feel bad, and I hate him."

"So that is your object, is it, Zeke?"

"You've got it."

"Well, whatever your motive may be, I shall be much obliged to you if you go. Here's ten cents for you!"

Zeke grasped at the coin with avidity, for his father was very parsimonious, and his mother no less so, and he seldom got any ready money.

"Thank you!" said Zeke, with unusual politeness. "I'll go right off. But, I say, don't you tell dad where I've gone, or he might prevent me, and don't you let on you've given me this dime, or he'd try to get it away."

"No, I won't say anything about it," answered Philip.

"A curious family this is!" he thought, "There doesn't seem to be much confidence in each other."

Zeke sauntered away carelessly, to avert suspicion but when he had got round a bend of the road he increased his speed, never looking back, lest he should see his father signaling for him.

Philip breathed a sigh of relief.

"I've got a messenger at last," he said. "Now my friends will know what has become of me when I don't come home to supper."

He was a little curious to learn what they were going to do with him, but he was not long kept in suspense.

CHAPTER X.

BAD TIDINGS.

Leaving Philip for a short time in the hands of his captor, we will follow Zeke on his errand. He didn't have to go as far as Mr. Dunbar's house, for he met Frank Dunbar about a quarter of a mile this side of it.

Now, between Frank Dunbar and Zeke Tucker there was no love lost. There had been a difficulty between them, originating at school, which need not be particularly referred to. Enough that it led to Zeke's cordially disliking Frank, while the latter, who was a frank, straightforward boy, could not see anything in Mr. Tucker's promising son to enlist either his respect or his liking.

There was a small river running through Norton, which crossed the main thoroughfare, and had to be bridged over. Frank Dunbar, fishing-line in hand, was leaning over the parapet, engaged in luring the fish from their river home. He looked up, when he saw Zeke approaching him. Not having any particular desire to hold a conversation with him, he withdrew his eyes, and again watched his line. Zeke, however, approached him with a grin of anticipated enjoyment, and hailed him in the usual style:

"Hello, Frank!"

"Oh, it's you, is it?" said Frank Dunbar indifferently.

"Yes it's me. I suppose you thought it was somebody else," chuckled Zeke, though Frank could see no cause for merriment.

"Well, I see who it is now," he responded.

"Where is Phil Gray?" inquired Zeke, chuckling again.

"Do you want to see him?" asked Frank, rather surprised.

"Oh, no! I shall see him soon enough."

And again Zeke chuckled.

Frank looked up.

He was expecting Philip to join him, and was, in fact, waiting for him now. Zeke's mysterious merriment suggested that he might have met Philip - possibly bore some message from him.

"Do you know anything about Phil?" asked Frank, looking fixedly at his visitor.

"I reckon I do. I know all about him," said Zeke, with evident enjoyment.

"Well. If you have any message from him, let me hear it."

"You can't guess where he is," blurted out Zeke.

"He isn't in any trouble, is he?" asked Frank quickly.

"No; he's safe enough. But you needn't expect to see him tonight."

"Why not?" demanded Frank, not yet guessing what was likely to detain his friend.

"Because he's at our house," chuckled Zeke. "Dad and Squire Pope have carried him to the poorhouse, and he's goin' to stay there for good."

This was a surprise. In his astonishment, Frank nearly let go his rod. He was eager now to question Zeke further.

"You don't mean to say Phil has been carried to the poorhouse against his will?" he exclaimed.

"I reckon he was anxious to go," said Zeke.

"Where was he when your father and Squire Pope committed this outrage?" said Frank indignantly.

"I thought you'd be mad," said Zeke, with the same unpleasant chuckle.

"Answer my question, or I'll pitch you into the river," said Frank sternly.

He did not mean what he said, but Zeke drew back in alarm.

"Quit now! I didn't have nothin' to do with it," said Zeke hastily. "Me and him was over in Haywood's pasture when dad come along with the squire in his wagon. Well, they made Phil get in, and that's all of it, except I promised I'd come and tell your folks, so you needn't get scared or nothin' when he didn't come back to-night."

"He will come back to-night," said Frank. "He won't stay in the poorhouse."

"Yes, he will. He can't help himself. Dad's goin' to lock him up in the attic. I guess he won't jump out of the window. Where you go-in'! You ain't got through fishin', be you?"

"Yes, I'm through," answered Frank, as he drew his line out of the water. "Just tell Phil when you go home that he's got friends outside who won't see him suffer."

"Say, ain't you goin' to give me nothin' for comin' to tell you!" asked Zeke, who was always intent on the main chance.

Frank flung a nickel in his direction, which Zeke picked up with avidity.

"I guess it pays to run errands when you can get paid twice," he reflected complacently.

Horatio Alger

CHAPTER XI.

PHILIP'S NEW ROOM.

We return to Phil.

"Foller me, boy!" said Mr. Tucker, as he entered the house, and proceeded to ascend the front steps.

Philip had formed his plans, and without a word of remonstrance, he obeyed. The whole interior was dingy and dirty. Mrs. Tucker was not a neat woman, and everything looked neglected and slipshod.

In the common room, to the right, the door of which was partly open, Philip saw some old men and women sitting motionless, in a sort of weary patience. They were "paupers," and dependent for comfort on the worthy couple, who regarded them merely as human machines, good to them for sixty cents a week each.

Mr. Tucker did not stop at the first landing, but turned and began to ascend a narrower and steeper staircase leading to the next story.

This was, if anything, dirtier and more squalid than the first and second. There were several small rooms on the third floor, into one of which Mr. Tucker pushed his way. "Come in," he said. "Now you're at home.

This is goin' to be your room."

Philip looked around him in disgust, which he did not even take the trouble to conceal.

There was a cot-bed in the corner, with an unsavory heap of bed-clothing upon it, and a couple of chairs, both with wooden seats, and one with the back gone.

That was about all the furniture. There was one window looking out upon the front.

"So this is to be my room, is it?" asked our hero.

"Yes. How do you like it?"

"I don't see any wash-stand, or any chance to wash."

"Come, that's rich!" said Mr. Tucker, appearing to be very much amused. "You didn't think you was stoppin' in the Fifth Avenoo Hotel, did you?"

"This don't look like it."

"We ain't used to fashionable boarders, and we don't know how to take care of 'em. You'll have to go down-stairs and wash in the trough, like the rest of the paupers do."

"And wipe my face on the grass, I suppose?" said Philip coolly, though his heart sank within him at the thought of staying even one night in a place so squalid and filthy.

"Come, that's goin' too far," said Mr. Tucker, who felt that the reputation of the boarding. house was endangered by such insinuations. "We mean to live respectable. There's two towels a week allowed, and that I consider liberal."

"And do all your boarders use the same towel?" asked Phil, unable to suppress an expression of disgust.

"Sartain. You don't think we allow 'em one apiece, do you!"

"No, I don't," said Philip decidedly.

He had ceased to expect anything so civilized in Mr. Tucker's establishment.

"Now you're safe in your room, I reckon I'd better go downstairs," said Tucker.

"I will go with you."

"Not much you won't! We ain't a-goin' to give you a chance of runnin' away just yet!"

"Do you mean to keep me a prisoner?" demanded Philip.

"That's just what we do, at present," answered his genial host.

"It won't be for long, Mr. Tucker."

"What's that you say? I'm master here, I'd have you to know!"

Just then a shrill voice was heard from below:

"Come down, Joe Tucker! Are you goin' to stay upstairs all day?"

"Comin', Abigail!" answered Mr. Tucker hastily, as he backed out of the room, locking the door behind him. Philip heard the click of the key as it turned in the lock, and he realized, for the first time in his life, that he was a prisoner.

CHAPTER XII.

A PAUPER'S MEAL

Half an hour later Philip heard a pounding on the door of his room.

He was unable to open it, but he called out, loud enough for the outsider to hear:

"Who is it?"

"It's me - Zeke," was the answer that came back.

"Did you tell the Dunbars where I was?" asked Philip eagerly.

"Yes."

"I shouldn't think you had time to go there and back," said Philip, fearing that Zeke had pocketed his money and then played him false. But, as we know, he was mistaken in this.

"I didn't go there," shouted Zeke. "I met Frank on the bridge."

"What did he say?"

"He was mad," answered Zeke, laughing. "I thought he would be."

"Did he send any message to me?" asked Philip.

"No; he stopped fishin' and went home." Here the conversation was interrupted. The loud tones in which Zeke had been speaking, in order to be heard through the door, had attracted attention below.

His father came to the foot of the attic stairs and demanded suspiciously:

"What you doin' there, Zeke?"

"Tryin' to cheer up Phil Gray," answered Zeke jocosely.

"He don't need any cheerin' up. He's all right. I reckon you're up to some mischief."

"No, I ain't."

"Come along down."

"All right, dad, if you say so. Lucky he didn't hear what I was sayin' about seein' Frank Dunbar," thought Zeke. "He'd be mad."

Presently there was another caller at Philip's room, or, rather, prison. This time it was Mr. Tucker himself. He turned the key in the lock and opened the door. Philip looked up inquiringly.

"Supper's ready," announced Joe. "You can come down if you want to."

Philip was provided with an appetite, but he did not relish the idea of going downstairs and joining the rest of Mr. Tucker's boarders. It would seem like a tacit admission that he was one of their number. Of course, he couldn't do without eating, but he had a large apple in his pocket when captured, and he thought that this would prevent his suffering from hunger for that night, at least, and he did not mean to spend another at the Norton poorhouse. The problem of to-morrow's supply of food might be deferred till then.

"I don't care for any supper," answered Philip.

"Perhaps you expect your meals will be brought up to you?" said Mr. Tucker, with a sneer.

"I haven't thought about it particularly," said Philip coolly.

"You may think you're spitin' me by not eatin' anything," observed Mr. Tucker, who was rather alarmed lest Philip might have made up his mind to starve himself.

This would be embarrassing, for it would make an investigation necessary.

"Oh, no," answered Philip, smiling; "that never came into my mind."

"I don't mind bringin' you up your supper for once," said Tucker. "Of course, I can't do it reg'lar, but this is the first night."

"I suppose I shall be better able to make my escape if I eat," thought Philip. "Probably the most sensible thing is to accept this offer."

"How much are you to get for my board, Mr. Tucker?" he asked.

"Only sixty cents," grumbled Tucker. "It ain't enough, but the town won't pay any more. You've no idea what appetites them paupers has."

"You made a mistake when you agreed to take me" said Philip gravely. "I'm very hearty, you'll be sure to lose money on me."

Mr. Tucker looked uneasy.

"Well, you see I expect to have you earn part of your board by doin' chores," he said, after a pause.

"That will give me a good chance to run away," remarked Philip calmly. "You'll have to let me out of this room to work, you know."

"You wouldn't dare to run away!" said Tucker, trying to frighten Philip by a blustering manner.

"That shows you don't know me, Mr. Tucker!" returned our hero. "I give you fair warning that I shall run away the first chance I get."

Philip's tone was so calm and free from excitement that Mr. Tucker could not help seeing that he was in earnest, and he looked perplexed.

"You don't look at it in the right light," he said, condescending to conciliate his new boarder. "If you don't make no trouble, you'll have a good time, and I'll let you off, now an' then, to play with Zeke. He needs a boy to play with."

Philip smiled, for the offer did not attract him very much.

"You are very kind," he said, "but I don't think that even that will reconcile me to staying here with you. But, if you'll agree to let me pay you for the supper, you may bring me up some."

"The town will pay me," said Tucker.

"That's just what I don't want the town to do," said Philip quickly. "I will make you an offer. At sixty cents a week the meals for one day will not cost over ten cents. I'll pay you ten cents for supper and breakfast."

"You're a cur'us boy," said Tucker. "You want to pay for your vittles in a free boardin'-house."

"It isn't free to me. At any rate, I don't want it to be. What do you say?"

"Oh, I ain't no objections to take your money," said Tucker, laughing. "I didn't know you was so rich."

"I am not rich, but I think I can pay my board as long as I stay here."

This Philip said because he had decided that his stay should be a very brief one.

"Just as you say!" chuckled Mr. Tucker.

As he went downstairs he reflected:

"I can take the boy's money and charge his board to the town, too. There's nothin' to hen-der, and it'll be so much more in my pocket. I wish the rest of the paupers would foller his example."

He went downstairs and explained to Mrs. Tucker that he wanted Philip's supper.

"Tell him to come down to the table like the rest of the folks!" retorted Mrs. Tucker. "He ain't too lazy, is he?"

"No; but it's safer to keep him in his room for the first twenty-four hours. He's a desperate boy, but I reckon he'll get tamed after a while."

"I'll desperate him!" said Mrs. Tucker scornfully. "I don't believe in humorin' him."

"Nor I, Abigail. He'd like to come down, but I won't let him. We can manage him between us."

"I should smile if we couldn't," said Mrs. Tucker. "If you want any supper for him, you can get it yourself. I've got too much to do. No, Widder Jones, you can't have another cup of tea, and you needn't beg for it. One clip's plenty for you, and it's all we can afford."

"Only this once," pleaded the poor old woman. "I've got a headache."

"Then another cup of tea would only make it worse. If you've got through your supper, go back to your seat and give more room for the rest."

While Mrs. Tucker was badgering and domineering over her regular boarders, her husband put two slices of dry bread on a plate, poured out a cup of tea, not strong enough to keep the most delicate child awake, and surreptitiously provided an extra luxury in the shape of a thin slice of cold meat. He felt that, as he was to receive double price, he ought to deal generously by our hero.

He carried this luxurious supper to the third story, and set it down before Philip.

Philip promptly produced a dime, which Mr. Tucker pocketed with satisfaction. He waited till his young guest had finished his repast, in order himself to carry down the dishes.

There was no butter for the bread, and the tea had been sweetened scantily. However, Philip had the appetite of a healthy boy, and he ate and drank everything that had been provided.

"I'll be up in the morning," said Mr. Tucker. "We go to bed early here. The paupers go to roost at seven, and me and my wife and Zeke at eight. You'd better go to bed early, too."

CHAPTER XIII.

A FRIENDLY MISSION.

Philip was glad to hear that all in the almshouse went to bed so early. He had not yet given up the hope of escaping that night, though he had as yet arranged no definite plan of escape.

Meanwhile, he had an active friend outside. I refer, of course, to Frank Dunbar. Frank had no sooner heard of his friend's captivity than he instantly determined, if it were a possible thing, to help him to escape.

He would not even wait till the next day, but determined after it was dark to visit the poor-house and reconnoiter. First, he informed his parents what had befallen Phil. Their indignation was scarcely less than his.

"Squire Pope is carrying matters with a high hand," said the farmer. "According to my idea, he has done no less than kidnap Philip, without the shadow of a legal right."

"Can't he be prosecuted?" asked Frank eagerly.

"I am not sure as to that," answered his father, "but I am confident that Philip will not be obliged to remain, unless he chooses, a dependent upon the charity of the town."

"It is outrageous!" said Mrs. Dunbar, who was quite as friendly to Philip as her husband and son.

"In my opinion," said Mr. Dunbar, "Squire Pope has done a very unwise thing as regards his own interests. He desires to remain in office, and the people will not be likely to reelect him if his policy is to make paupers of those who wish to maintain themselves. Voters will be apt to think that they are sufficiently taxed already for the support of those who are actually unable to maintain themselves."

"If I were a voter," exclaimed Frank indignantly, "I wouldn't vote for Squire Pope, even for dog-catcher! The meanest part of it is the underhanded way in which he has taken Phil. He must have known he was acting illegally, or he would have come here in open day and required Phil to go with him."

"I agree with you, Frank. Squire Pope may be assured that he has lost my vote from henceforth. Hitherto I have voted for him annually for selectman, knowing that he wanted the office and considering him fairly faithful."

"Father," said Frank, after a thoughtful pause, "do you think Philip would be justified in escaping from the poorhouse?"

"I do," answered Mr. Dunbar. "In this free country I hold that no one ought to be made an object of charity against his will."

"Philip is strong enough and smart enough to earn his own living," said Frank.

"That is true. I will myself give him his board and clothes if he will stay with me and work on the farm."

"I wish he would. He would be a splendid companion for me; but I think he wants to leave Norton, and try his fortune in some larger place."

"I can't blame him. If his father were living and he had a good home, I should not think it wise; but, as matters stand, it may not be a bad plan for him."

"Father," said Frank, after supper, "I am going out and I may not be back very early."

"Are you going to see Philip?"

"Yes; but I want to see him alone. If possible, I will see him without attracting the attention of Joe Tucker."

"You won't get into any trouble, Frank?" said his mother anxiously.

"No, mother; I don't know what trouble I can get into."

"You may very likely fail to see Philip," suggested his father. "I hear that Tucker and his boarders go to bed very early."

"So much the better!" said Frank, in a tone of satisfaction. "The only one I want to see is Philip, and he isn't likely to go to sleep very early."

Mr. Dunbar smiled to himself.

"Frank has got some plan in his head," he thought. "I won't inquire what it is, for he has good common sense, and won't do anything improper."

About eight o'clock, Frank, after certain preparations, which will hereafter be referred to, set out for the poorhouse, which was about a mile distant,

CHAPTER XIV.

PHILIP MAKES HIS ESCAPE.

It grew darker and darker in Philip's chamber, but no one came to bring him a light. It was assumed that he would go to bed before he required one.

By seven o'clock the paupers had settled themselves for the night, and when eight o'clock struck, Mr. and Mrs. Tucker sought their beds. It was no particular trial for Joe Tucker to go to bed early, for he was naturally a lazy man, and fond of rest; while his wife, who worked a great deal harder than he, after being on her feet from four o'clock in the morning, found it a welcome relief to lie down and court friendly sleep. Zeke wasn't always ready to go to bed. In fact, he would much rather have gone up to the village now and then, but if he had done so he would have had to stay out all night. There was one thing his parents were strict about, and that was retiring at eight o'clock.

Philip, however, did not retire at that hour. It was earlier than his usual hour for bed. Besides, he was in hopes his friend Frank would make his appearance, and help him, though he didn't exactly understand how, to make his escape.

At half-past eight it was dark. The stars were out, and

the moon was just making its appearance. Philip had opened his window softly, and was looking out, when all at once he saw a boyish figure approaching.

Couldn't be Frank Dunbar.

He hoped so, but in the indistinct light could not be quite certain.

The boy, whoever it might be, approached cautiously, till he stood within fifty feet of the house.

Then Philip saw that it was indeed Frank, and his heart beat joyfully. It was something to see a friend, even though they were separated by what seemed to him to be an impassable gulf.

About the same time, Frank recognized his friend, in the boyish figure at the window.

"Is that you, Phil?" he asked, in a guarded voice, yet loud enough to be heard.

"Yes, Frank; I have been expecting you. I knew you wouldn't desert me."

"I should think not. I didn't come before, because I didn't want to be seen by any of Tucker's folks."

"They are all abed now, and I hope asleep."

"Can't you come downstairs, and steal away?"

"No; my chamber door is locked on the outside."

"That's what I thought."

"Can't you help me in any way?"

"I'll see. Suppose you had a rope - could you swing out of the window?"

"Yes; I could fasten it to the bedstead, and fix that just against the window."

"Then I think I can help you. Can you catch a ball?"

"Yes; but what good will that do?"

"You'll see. Make ready now, and don't miss it."

He produced a ball of common size, and after taking aim, threw it lightly up toward Philip's window. The first time it didn't come within reach. The second Philip caught it skilfully, and by the moonlight saw that a stout piece of twine was attached to it. At the end of the twine Frank had connected it with a clothesline which he had borrowed from home.

"Now pull away, Phil," urged Frank.

Philip did, and soon had the stout line in his possession.

"It will hold; it's new and strong," said Frank. "Father only bought it last week. I didn't think, then, what use we should have for it."

Philip, however, was not afraid. He was so anxious to escape that, even if there had been any risk to run, he would readily have incurred it for the sake of getting away from the poor-house, in which he was unwilling to spend a single night. He fastened one end of the rope firmly to his bedstead, as he had proposed, then cautiously got upon the window-sill and lowered himself, descending hand over hand till he reached the ground.

He breathed a sigh of relief as he detached himself from the rope and stood beside Frank Dunbar.

Just then the boys heard a second-story window open, and saw Mr. Tucker's head projecting from it.

CHAPTER XV.

ESCAPE AND FLIGHT.

Though the boys had made as little noise as possible, conversing in an undertone, they had been heard by Mrs. Tucker. Her husband, as was his custom, had gone to sleep; but Mrs. Tucker, who, during the day, had discovered the loss of ten cents from her bureau drawer in which she kept her savings, had been kept awake by mental trouble. Some of my readers may think so small a loss scarcely worth keeping awake for, but Mrs. Joe Tucker was a strictly economical and saving woman - some even called her penurious - and the loss of ten cents troubled her.

She would have laid it to one of "them paupers," as she was wont contemptuously to refer to them, except that she never allowed one of them to enter the sacred precincts of her chamber.

A horrible thought entered her mind. Could it be Zeke, the boy whom she thought such a paragon, though no one else had been able to discover his virtues or attractions! She did not like to think of it, but it did occur to her that Zeke, the previous day, had asked her for ten cents, though he would not own the purpose for which he wanted it. The boy might have been tempted to take the money. At any rate, she would go and see.

Zeke slept in a small room adjoining. When his mother entered, with a candle in her hand, he was lying asleep, with his mouth wide open, and one arm dropped over the side of the bed.

Mrs. Tucker took a look at him, and saw that he was wrapped in slumber and unable to notice what she proposed to do. His clothes were thrown down carelessly on a chair near-by.

Mrs. Tucker searched first in the pockets of his pants, and, though she discovered a large variety of miscellaneous articles, "of no use to any one except the owner," she didn't discover any traces of the missing dime. She began to hope that he had not taken it, after all, although, in that case, the loss would continue to be shrouded in obscurity. But, on continuing her search, she discovered in one of the pockets of his vest a silver ten-cent piece.

Mrs. Tucker's eyes flashed, partly with indignation at Zeke's dishonesty, partly with joy at the recovery of the missing coin.

"I've found you out, you bad boy!" she said, in a low voice, shaking her fist at the sleeping boy. "I wouldn't have believed that my Zeke would have robbed his own mother. We must have a reckoning to-morrow."

She was half-inclined to wake Zeke up and charge him with his crime, confronting him with the evidence of it which she had just discovered; but on second thoughts she decided that she might as well let him sleep, as the next day would do just as well.

Poor Zeke! he was not guilty, after all, though whether

his honesty was strict enough to resist a powerful temptation, I am not sure.

The dime which Mrs. Tucker had discovered was the same one that Philip had given to Zeke in return for his service in notifying Frank Dunbar of his captivity. In another pocket was the five-cent piece given him by Frank, but that had escaped his mother's attention.

The reader will understand now how it happened that Mrs. Tucker was kept awake beyond her usual time. She was broad awake when Frank Dunbar arrived, and she heard something through the partially open window of the conference between the two boys. She heard the voices that is to say, but could not tell what was said.

With her mind dwelling upon Zeke's supposed theft, however, she was more easily frightened than usual, and immediately jumped to the conclusion that there were burglars outside, trying to get in.

The absurdity of burglars attempting to rob the town poorhouse did not occur to her in panic. She sat up in bed, and proceeded to nudge her husband in no gentle fashion.

"Mr. Tucker!" she exclaimed.

Her husband responded by an inarticulate murmur, but did not wake.

"Mr. Tucker!" she exclaimed, in a louder voice, giving him a still more vigorous shake.

"Eh! What! What's the matter?" said Tucker, opening

his eyes at last, and staring vacantly at his wife.

"What's the matter!" retorted his wife impatiently. "The matter is that there's burglars outside!"

"Let 'em stay outside!" said Joe Tucker, in a sleepy tone.

"Did any one ever hear such a fool?" exclaimed Mrs. Tucker, exasperated. "They're trying to get in. Do you hear that, Mr. Tucker?"

"Trying to get in! Is the door locked?" asked Joe, a little alarmed.

"You must get up and defend the house," continued Mrs. Tucker.

Now, Mr. Tucker was not a brave man. He had no fancy for having a hand-to-hand conflict with burglars, who might be presumed to be desperate men. It occurred to him that it would be decidedly better to stay where he was and ran no risk.

"Never mind, Abigail," he said, soothingly. "The burglars can't do us any harm. They ean't do any more than carry off a pauper or two, and I don't, believe they'll do that."

"I wouldn't mind that, Mr. Tucker; but I've left the spoons down-stairs!" answered his wife.

"How many are there!"

"Six. I want you to go down and get them and bring them up here, where they will be safe."

"But suppose I should meet some of the burglars!" suggested Tucker, trembling.

"Then you must defend yourself like a man!"

"You might find me in the morning weltering in my gore!" said Joe, with an uneasy shudder.

"Are we to have the spoons stolen, then!" demanded Mrs. Tucker sharply.

"If you care so much for the spoons, Abigail, you'd better go down-stairs yourself and get 'em. I don't value them as much as my life."

"I don't know but I will, if you'll look out of the window and see whether you can see any of the burglars outside," responded Mrs. Tucker. "If they haven't got in yet, I'll take the risk."

"Where did you hear 'em, Abigail?"

"Eight outside. Open the window and look out, and you may see 'em."

Mr. Tucker was not entirely willing to do this, but still he preferred it to going down-stairs after the spoons, and accordingly he advanced, and, lifting the window, put his head out, as described at the close of the last chapter.

Philip and Frank were just ready to go when they heard the window rising, and naturally looked up in some trepidation.

"It's old Tucker!" said Frank, in a low voice.

Philip looked up, and saw that his friend was right.

Mr. Tucker had not yet discovered them, but the whisper caught his ear, and looking down he caught sight of the two boys.

In his alarm, and the obscurity of the night, he did not make out that they were boys and not men, and was about to withdraw his head in alarm, when a mischievous impulse seized Frank Dunbar.

"Give me the ball, Philip!" he said quickly.

Philip complied with his request, not understanding his intention.

Now, Frank belonged to a baseball club, and had a capital aim. He threw up the ball and struck Mr. Tucker fairly in the nose. The effect upon the terrified Joe was startling.

Full as his mind was of burglars, he fancied that it was something a great deal more deadly that had struck him.

"Oh, Abigail! I'm shot through the brain!" he moaned in anguish, as he poked in his head and fell back upon the floor.

"What do you mean, Joe?" asked his wife, in alarm, as she hastened to her prostrate husband, whose hand was pressed convulsively upon the injured organ, which, naturally ached badly with the force of the blow.

"I'm a dead man!" moaned Mr. Tucker; "and it's all your fault. You made me go to the window."

"I don't believe you're shot at all! I didn't hear any report," said Mrs. Tucker. "Let me see your face."

Mr. Tucker withdrew his hand mournfully.

"You've only been struck with a rock or something," said she, after a careful examination.

"It's bleeding!" groaned Job, seeing a dark stain on his night-dress.

"Suppose it is - it won't kill you. I'll look out myself."

But she saw nothing. Philip and Frank had immediately taken to flight, and vanished in the darkness.

"They've run away!" announced Mrs. Tucker. "My spoons are safe."

"But my nose isn't," groaned Mr. Tucker.

"You won't die this time," said Mrs. Tucker, not very sympathetically. "Soak your nose in the wash-basin, and you'll be all right in the morning."

The two boys were destined to have another adventure that night.

CHAPTER XVI.

A NIGHT ADVENTURE.

"I didn't mean to hit him," said Frank, as he and Philip hurried away from the poorhouse, "I only intended to give him a fright."

"I think you have. I wonder whether he recognized us!"

"I don't believe it. He had hardly got his head out of the window before I let drive."

"Then he won't imagine I have escaped."

"What are your plans, Phil? Suppose they try to take you back to the poorhouse?"

"They won't get the chance. Before five o'clock to-morrow morning I shall leave Norton."

"Leave town?" exclaimed Frank, in surprise. "And so soon?"

"Yes. There is nothing for me to do here."

"Father would like to have you stay and assist him on the farm. He said so to me. He wouldn't be able to pay much, but I think we would have a good time together."

Philip pressed his friend's hand warmly.

"I know we should, Frank," he said, "but if I remained here, it would only remind me of my poor father. I would rather go out into the world and try my fortune."

"Isn't it risky, Phil?" objected Frank doubtfully.

"I suppose it is; but I am willing to work, and I don't expect much."

"Suppose you fall sick?"

"Then, if I can, I will come back to you and your good father and mother, and stay till I am well."

"Promise me that, Phil?"

"I promise."

"I wish I could go with you, Phil," said Frank, with a boyish impulse.

"No, it wouldn't be wise for you. You have a good home, and you will be better off there than among strangers."

"It might be your home, too, Phil."

"Thank you; but I shall be better away from Norton for a time."

A minute later, Frank said suddenly:

"There's Squire Pope coming. He will see you."

"I don't care. He won't take me back."

"Get behind the stone wall, and I will wait and interview him."

Philip immediately followed the advice of his friend. He was curious to hear what the squire would say.

Squire Pope's eyesight was not good, and it was only when he came near that he recognized Frank Dunbar. He stopped short, for there was a subject on which he wished to speak.

"Frank Dunbar!" he said.

"Do you wish to speak to me, sir?" inquired Frank coldly.

"Yes. Where have you been?"

"Out walking," answered Frank shortly.

"Have you been to the poorhouse?"

"I have."

"Did you see Philip?"

"I saw him looking out of a third-story window."

Squire Pope chuckled, if, indeed, such a dignified man can be said to chuckle.

"What did he say?" he condescended to inquire.

"That he wouldn't stay."

"He will have to," responded Squire Pope complacently. "Mr. Tucker will see to that."

"Probably Mr. Tucker will wake up some fine morning and find Phil's room empty," said Frank quietly.

"I'll take the risk of it," returned the squire serenely. "But there's a matter I want to speak to you about. You've got Philip's fiddle in your possession."

"Suppose I have."

"I wish you to bring it round to my house in the morning, and I'll give you something for your trouble."

"You must excuse me, Squire Pope. If it were your property, I would bring it to you and charge nothing for my trouble."

"Young man," said the squire sternly. "I am Philip's legal guardian, and I have a right to receive his violin. You will get into trouble if you resist my authority."

"If you will give me Philip's order for it, you shall have it, sir."

"Frank Dunbar, you are trifling with me. Philip is now a pauper, and has no right to hold property of any kind. He cannot give a legal order."

"Then you are guardian to a pauper?"

"In my capacity of overseer of the poor."

"In my capacity as Philip's friend, I refuse to consider you his guardian. You may call him a pauper, but that doesn't make him one."

"He is an inmate of the Norton Poorhouse."

Frank laughed.

"I don't want to be disrespectful, Squire Pope," he said; "but I can't help telling you that you undertook a bigger job than you thought for, when you made up your mind to make a pauper of Philip Gray."

Squire Pope was indignant at the coolness of Frank.

"I shall come to your house to-morrow morning," he said, "and convince you to the contrary."

"Very well, sir."

Frank Dunbar bowed, and the squire went his way.

"That's a very impudent boy!" he soliloquized. "Just like the Gray boy. It wouldn't do him any harm to put him under Joe Tucker's care, too."

After the squire had passed on, Philip came out from behind the stone wall.

"Did you hear what passed between your guardian and myself?" asked Frank.

"Yes, I heard every word."

"He little thought that the bird had flown, Phil."

"He will make all the trouble he can. That is one more reason why I think it best to leave town."

"I wouldn't let Squire Pope drive you out of town."

"I would stay and face the music if it suited me, but I want to go away."

"Suppose we cut across this field. It will be a little nearer."

"All right."

There was a pathway through a pasture-lot, comprising some ten acres, poor land, covered with puny bushes, and a few gnarled trees, producing cider-apples. It belonged to an old bachelor farmer, who lived in solitary fashion, doing his own cooking, and in general taking care of himself. He was reputed to have money concealed about his premises, which was quite probable, as he spent little, and was known to have received, four years before, a considerable legacy from the estate of a brother who had died, a successful merchant in the city of New York.

The boys had to pass by the small and weather-stained house where he lived, as the path ran very near it.

When within a few rods of the house, the boys were startled by a sharp cry of terror, which appeared to proceed from inside the house.

Both simultaneously stood still.

"What's that!" exclaimed both in concert.

"Somebody must be trying to rob Mr. Lovett," suggested Frank.

"Can't we do something!" said Phil quickly.

"We can try."

There were two stout sticks or clubs lying on the ground at their feet. They stooped, picked them up, and ran to the house. A glance showed that one of the windows on the north side had been raised.

The window sill was low. Pausing a moment before springing over it into the room, they looked in and this was what they saw:

The farmer lay half-prostrate on the floor, half supporting himself by a chair, which he had mechanically grasped as he was forced downward. Over him stood a ruffianly looking tramp, whom Phil remembered to have seen about the streets during the day, with a stick uplifted. He had not heard the approach of the boys.

"Give me two hundred dollars, and I'll go," he said to the man at his feet.

"I cannot do it. I haven't got as much here."

"That's a lie!" said the other coarsely. "I heard all about you to-day. You're a miser, and you've got no end of money stowed away here. Get it for me, quick, or I'll dash your brains out."

Just then the prostrate farmer saw what the tramp could not see, his back being turned to the window, the faces of the two boys looking through the window. Fresh courage came to him. Single-handed, and taken at advantage, he was no match for the ruffian who had entered his house; but with these two young auxiliaries he felt that all was not lost.

CHAPTER XVII.

A REFORMED BURGLAR.

"What do you say!" demanded the tramp impatiently. "Speak quick! I can't stay here all night."

"Let me up, and I'll see if I can find the money for you."

"I thought I'd bring you to terms," said the tramp, laughing grimly.

He allowed his victim to rise, as he certainly would not have done if he had looked behind him and seen the two boys at the window.

"Now's our time," answered Philip.

He gave a light spring into the room, followed by Frank.

Of course, the tramp heard them, and turned in sudden alarm. As he turned, the farmer snatched the club from his hand, and he found himself unexpectedly unarmed and confronted by three enemies.

"It's my turn now," said Lovett. "Do you surrender?"

The tramp saw that the game was up and made a dash for the open window, but Philip skillfully inserted a stick between his legs, and tripped him up, and, with the help of Mr. Lovett, held him, struggling desperately, till Frank fetched a rope, with which he was securely bound.

"Confound you!" he said, scowling at the two boys. "But for you I would have succeeded and got away with my booty."

"That's true!" said the farmer. "I owe my escape from robbery, and, perhaps, bodily injury, to you."

"I am glad we were at hand," said Philip.

"And now, my friend," said the farmer, "I may as well say that you were quite mistaken in supposing I kept a large amount of money in this lonely house. I should be a fool to do it, and I am not such a fool as that."

"Where do you keep your money, then?" growled the tramp.

"In different savings-banks. I am ready to tell you, for it will do you no good."

"I wish I'd known it sooner. I came here on a fool's errand."

"I am glad you have found it out."

"Now, what are you going to do with me!"

"Keep you here till I can deliver you into the hands of the law."

Horatio Alger

"That won't do you any good."

"It will give you a home, where you cannot prey on the community."

"I don't mean to do so any more. I'm going to turn over a new leaf and become an honest man - that is, if you'll let me go."

"Your conversion is rather sudden. I haven't any faith in it."

"Listen to me," said the man, "and then decide. Do you think I am a confirmed lawbreaker?"

"You look like it."

"Yes, I do; but I am not. Never in my life have I been confined in any prison or penitentiary. I have never been arrested on any charge. I see you don't believe me. Let me tell you how I came to be what I am: Two years since I was a mechanic, tolerably well-to-do, owning a house with a small mortgage upon it. It was burned to the ground one night. I built another, but failed to insure it. Six months since, that, too, burned down, and left me penniless and in debt. Under this last blow I lost all courage. I left the town where I had long lived, and began a wandering life. In other words, I became a tramp. Steadily I lost my self-respect till I was content to live on such help as the charitable chose to bestow on me. It was not until to-day that I formed the plan of stealing. I heard in the village that you kept a large sum of money in your house, and an evil temptation assailed me. I had become tired of wandering, and determined to raise a sum which would enable me to live at ease for a time, I should have succeeded but for these two boys."

"And you are sorry you did not succeed?"

"I was, five minutes since, but I feel differently now. I have been saved from crime. Now, I have told you my story. Do with me as you will."

The man's appearance was rough, but there was something in his tone which led Mr. Lovett to think that he was speaking the truth.

"Boys," he said, "you have heard what this man says. What do you think of it?"

"I believe him!" said Philip promptly.

"Thank you, boy," said the tramp. "I am glad some one has confidence in me."

"I believe you, too," said Frank.

"I have not deceived you. Your words have done me more good than you think. It is my first attempt to steal, and it shall be my last."

"If you want to become an honest man, God forbid that I should do aught to prevent you!" said the farmer. "I may be acting unwisely, but I mean to cut this rope and let you go."

"Will you really do this?" said the tramp, his face lighting up with mingled joy and surprise.

"I will."

He knelt on the floor, and drawing from his pocket a large jack-knife, cut the rope.

The tramp sprang to his feet.

"Thank you," he said, in a husky voice. "I believe you are a good man. There are not many who would treat me as generously, considering what I tried to do just now. You sha'n't repent it. Will you give me your hand!"

"Gladly," said the farmer; and he placed his hand in that of the visitor, lately so unwelcome. "I wish you better luck."

"Boys, will you give me your hands, too?" asked tke tramp, turning to Philip and Frank.

Tke boys readily complied with his request, and repeated the good wishes of the farmer.

The stranger was about to leave the house, when Lovett said:

"Stay, my friend, I wish to ask you a question."

"Very well, sir."

"Have you any money?"

"Not a cent."

"Then take this," said the farmer, drawing from his vest pocket a five-dollar bill. "I lend it to you. Some time you will be able to repay it, if you keep to your resolution of leading an honest life. When that time comes, lend it to some man who needs it as you do now."

"Thank you, sir. I will take it, for it will help me greatly at this time. Good-by! If you ever see me again, you will see a different man."

He leaped through the window and was gone.

"I don't know if I have done a wise thing, but I will take the risk," said the farmer. "And now, boys, I want to make you some return for your assistance to-night." Both Frank and Philip earnestly protested that they would receive nothing in the conversation that ensued. Philip made known his intention to leave Norton the next morning.

"What are your plans? Where do you mean to go?" asked the farmer.

"I don't know, sir. I shall make up my mind as I go along. I think I can make my living somehow."

"Wait here five minutes," said Lovett, and he went into an adjoining room.

Within the time mentioned, he returned, holding in his hand a sealed letter.

"Philip," he said, "put this envelope in your pocket, and don't open it till you are fifty miles from here."

"Very well, sir," answered Philip, rather puzzled, but not so much surprised as he might have been if he had not known the farmer's reputation for eccentricity.

"I suppose it contains some good advice," he thought. "Well, good advice is what I need."

The two boys went home immediately upon leaving the farmhouse. Though so much had happened, it was not late, being not quite half-past nine.

Philip received a cordial welcome from Mr. and Mrs. Dunbar, who, however, hardly expected to see him so soon. "Are you willing to receive a pauper beneath your roof?" asked Philip, smiling.

"That you will never be while you have health and strength, I'll be bound," said Mr. Dunbar. "I like your pride and independence, Philip."

They tried to induce Philip to give up his resolution to leave Norton the next morning, but did not succeed.

"I will come back some time," he said. "Now I feel better to go."

At five o'clock the next morning, with a small bundle swung over his shoulder, attached to a stick, Philip Gray, carrying his violin, left the village, which, for some years, had been his home. Frank accompanied him for the first mile of his journey. Then the two friends shook hands and parted - not without sorrow, for who could tell when they would meet again?

CHAPTER XVIII.

A PROFESSIONAL ENGAGEMENT.

A depressing feeling of loneliness came to Phil after he had parted with Frank. He was going out into the world with no one to lean upon, and no one to sympathize with him or lend him a helping hand. No wonder he felt friendless and alone. But this mood did not last long.

"I shall find friends if I deserve them," he reflected, "and I don't mean to do anything dishonorable or wrong. I am willing to work, and I believe I can make a living."

Leaving him to proceed, we go back to the poor-house, where his absence was not noticed till morning.

Job Tucker, in spite of the blow which his nasal organ had received, slept pretty comfortably, and was awakened at an early hour by his vigilant spouse.

"You'd better go up and wake that boy and set him to work, Mr. Tucker," she said. "There are plenty of chores for him to do."

"You are right, Abigail," said Mr. Tucker, with approval. He reflected that he could assign to Philip some of the work which generally fell to himself, and the reflection was an agreeable one. He had tried to get work out of Zeke, but he generally found that it was harder to keep him at work than it was to do the job himself.

After he had made his toilet - not a very elaborate one - Mr. Tucker went up-stairs to arouse his young prisoner. He found the key in the outside of the door. Everything seemed right.

"I wonder how he feels this morning?" chuckled Mr. Tucker. "Wonder whether he's tamed down a little?"

He turned the key in the lock and threw open the door. He glanced at the bed, started in amazement to find that it had not been slept in, and then his wonder ceased, for the telltale rope explained how the boy had escaped.

He ran down-stairs in anger and excitement.

"What's the matter with you, Joe Tucker?" demanded his wife. "Are you drunk or crazy?"

"Enough to make me both, wife," he answered. "The boy's gone!"

"Gone!" exclaimed Mrs. Tucker, stopping short, with a saucepan in her hand.

"Gone!" ejaculated Zeke, his mouth wide open.

"I don't believe it," said Mrs. Tucker positively. "He couldn't go. He'd have to jump out of the third-story window."

"Sure enough!" said Zeke.

"I can't help it - he's gone," declared Mr. Tucker. "He tied a clothesline to the bedstead and let himself down from the window. Now, I want to know who left a clothesline in the room?"

"There wasn't any," said Mrs. Tucker.

"Maybe he had one in his pocket," suggested Zeke.

But this suggestion was not considered worthy of notice by his parents.

"Now I know who hit me in the nose!" exclaimed Mr. Tucker, light flashing upon him. "There was two of 'em - the ones I took for burglars."

"Then the other one must have been Frank Dunbar," said Mrs. Tucker.

"Zeke," said his father, "go right off and tell Squire Pope that Philip Gray has escaped. Ask him if I can't have him arrested for assault and battery. It's likely he's at Frank Dunbar's now. We'll have him back before the day is out, and then I'll see he don't get out!"

"All right, dad! As soon as I've had breakfast I'll go."

The result of Zeke's message was that Squire Pope hurried over to the poorhouse and held a conference with Mr. and Mrs. Tucker.

The next step was that he and Joe rode over to Mr. Dunbar's, to demand the return of the fugitive.

They found Frank splitting wood in the yard. To him they made known their errand, requesting him to call Philip out.

"He isn't here," answered Frank.

"Isn't here? I don't believe it!" said the squire hastily.

"Sorry you doubt my word, Squire Pope, but it's just as I say."

"Where is he, then?" demanded the squire suspiciously.

"He has left town."

"Left town?" repeated the squire and Joe Tucker, in dismay. "Where is he gone!"

"He's probably ten miles away by this time," answered Frank, enjoying their perplexity. "I guess you'd better wait till he comes back."

Job and the squire conferred together, but no satisfactory result was arrived at, except it wouldn't pay to pursue Philip, for two reasons - one, because they were quite uncertain in what direction he had gone; another, because, even if overtaken, they would have no authority to apprehend him, since he had been guilty of no crime.

Finally a bright idea came to the squire.

"Bring me out his fiddle," he said to Frank. "I'm his guardian, and I will take care of it for him."

"He carried it away with him," said Frank. The squire's lower jaw fell. He was defeated at all points. "I guess we can't do nothing, under the circumstances, squire," said Job Tucker, scratching his head.

"I shall have to reflect upon it," said Squire Pope, in a crestfallen tone.

"That's as good as a circus," thought Frank, as his roguish glance followed the two baffled conspirators as they rode out of the yard. "It's a pity Phil was not here to enjoy it."

At the end of the second day, Philip was some forty miles distant from Norton. He had not walked all the way, but had got a lift for a few miles from a tin-peddler, with whom he had a social chat.

It cannot be said that he was depressed, or that he regretted having left Norton, but he certainly did feel uncomfortable, and his discomfort sprang from a very homely cause.

To tell the plain truth, he was hungry. He had not had anything to eat for six hours except an apple, which he had picked up by the roadside, and during those six hours he had walked not far from fifteen miles.

"I believe I never was so hungry before," thought Philip. "The question is, where is my supper to come from?"

Although he knew pretty well the state of his finances, he began to search his pockets to see if he could not somewhere find a stray dime, or, better still, a quarter, with which to purchase the meal of which he stood so much in need. But his search was unproductive, or, rather, it only resulted in the discovery of a battered cent.

"So that penny constitutes my whole fortune," thought Philip.

There were two houses in sight, one on each side of the road.

Probably they would have given Philip a supper at either, but our hero's honest pride revolted at the idea of begging for a meal, much as he stood in need of it. He might as well be a pauper, as he justly reflected. So he pushed on.

Evidently he was drawing near a village, for houses began to appear at nearer intervals.

"Hello, my boy! Where are you traveling!" asked a hearty voice.

Philip turned round, and his glance rested on a stout young farmer, whose face, though very much sun-burned, was pleasant and good-natured.

"I don't know," answered Philip.

"Don't know?" was repeated in surprise.

"I am in search of work."

"Oh, that's it! Are you a musician?" asked the young man, looking at the violin.

"Yes; a little of one."

"Are you looking for a job at fiddling?" asked the young man.

"Yes, if I can find one," answered Philip, smiling.

"Can you play dancing-music?"

"Yes."

"Then I guess I can get you a job for this evening."

"I wish you could," said Philip hopefully, catching at a way out of his troubles.

"You see, there's to be a little dance in School-house Hall to-night," said the farmer; "or there was to be one, but the fiddler's took sick, and we was afraid we'd have to give it up. Now, if you'll take his place, we can have it, after all."

"I'll do it," said Philip promptly.

"What'll you charge?"

"How much was the other one going to charge?"

"Five dollars. You see, he would have to come six miles."

"I'll come for three dollars and my supper and lodging," said Philip.

"All right! You shall have supper and lodging at our house. There it is, down that lane. Come right along, for supper must be on the table. After supper I'll go and tell the committee I've engaged you."

Philip's spirits rose. Help had come from an unexpected quarter. He felt that a new career was opening before him.

CHAPTER XIX.

NEW ACQUAINTANCES.

On his way to the farmhouse, Philip ascertained that his companion's name was Abner Webb, and that he and his brother Jonas carried on a farm of about a hundred acres. Abner appeared to be about twenty-five years old.

"You seem pretty young to be a fiddler," said the young man, surveying Philip with a glance of curiosity.

"I am almost sixteen."

"I am twenty-five, and I can't play at all."

"It isn't all in the age," returned our hero. "Did you ever try to learn?"

"Yes, I took one or two lessons, but I had to give it up for a bad job. I couldn't get into it somehow."

"You didn't try very long," said Philip, smiling.

"I reckon I'd never do much at it. How long have you been a fiddler?"

"I've been playing three or four years."

"Sho! You don't say so! Do you like it?"

"Yes; very much."

"Well, I'm glad you happened along. It would have been a pity to have our dance spoiled."

By this time they had reached the farmhouse, and Abner went in, followed by our hero.

A young woman, his brother's wife, looked at Philip in some surprise.

"You see, I've got a fiddler, after all," said Abner gleefully. "We won't have to put off the dance."

As he spoke, his brother Jonas came into the room, and the explanation was repeated.

"That's good," said Jonas heartily. "You'd better go down to the store after supper, Abner, and tell the boys, for they've just heard that Paul Beck can't come."

"You just save me some supper, and I'll go now. The boy'll stay with us to-night. That's the bargain I made with him."

"He's heartily welcome," said Jonas Webb, a pleasant-faced man, with sandy complexion, who was probably from two to three years older than his brother. "You've happened along just at the right time."

"I am glad of it," said Philip; and there is no doubt he was sincere, for we know how much he stood in need of employment, though he naturally did not care to let his new friends know of his destitution.

"My brother didn't tell me your name," said Jonas.

"My name is Philip Gray," answered our hero.

"Do you go round playing for dances?" inquired Jonas.

"I have only just begun."

Philip didn't think it necessary to say that the idea of making money in this way had never occurred to him till this very day.

"Sit right up to supper, Jonas, and you, too, Mr. Gray," said Mrs. Webb.

Philip was by no means loath, for the dishes which he saw on the table had had the effect of stimulating his appetite, already sharpened by his long walk and long fast.

Philip, as the guest, was first helped to a bountiful supply of cold meat, a hot biscuit, and some golden butter, not to mention two kinds of preserves, for the Webbs always lived well. He was not slow in doing justice to the good supper spread before him. He was almost afraid to eat as much as he wanted, lest his appetite should attract attention, and, therefore, was pleased to see that Jonas quite kept pace with him.

Indeed, when he had already eaten as much as he dared, Mrs. Webb said, hospitably:

"I am afraid, Mr. Gray, you won't make out a supper."

"I don't think there is any danger of that," said Philip, smiling. "I have enjoyed my supper very much."

The young woman looked gratified by this tribute to her cooking, and just then Abner came in.

"Did you see the boys, Abner?" asked Jonas.

"Yes, I saw them all. They were awfully glad we could have the dance, after all. You see, we've been lookin' forward to it, and didn't like to be disappointed. And now I must hurry down my supper, for I've got to slick up and go for Mary Ann Temple. Are you goin', Lucy?"

"Of course she is," answered Jonas. "I don't have so far to go for my girl as you do," he added slyly.

"You used to go farther once, Jonas - six miles, where I have only to go two."

When supper was over, Philip inquired:

"How early will the dance commence?"

"About eight. We keep early hours in the country, and we like to get our money's worth."

"If you have no objection, I will go out to the barn and try my violin a little to see if it is in good tune."

"Try it in the next room," said the farmer's wife.

"Yes, do!" said her husband. "We'd like to hear you."

He was a little afraid, judging from Philip's youth, that

he could not play very well, and this would give him an opportunity of deciding how competent the boy was to take the place of Paul Beck, of Pomfret, who had quite a reputation in the towns around.

Philip went into the next room and began to prepare himself for his evening's task. Though lus training had by no means been confined to dancing-tunes, he was quite proficient in that department, having more than once been called upon in Norton to officiate in a similar capacity.

When Jonas had listened for five minutes to Philip, he turned to Abner with a satisfied look.

"He understands his business," he said, nodding with emphasis. "He ain't no new beginner."

"I think he beats Paul Beck," said Abner, delighted to find his choice approved.

"I don't know but he does. I feel as if I wanted to start off now."

"I don't see how he does it," said Abner, with a puzzled look. "I never could do anything at it, though I'm almost twice as old."

He passed into the room where Philip was practising.

"You're a tip-top player," said he, to Philip admiringly. "Why, you beat Paul Beck."

"Is he the one you expected to have?"

"Yes. Paul's got a big name for fiddlin'."

"I am glad you like my playing," said Philip, who was naturally pleased to find that he was likely to give satisfaction in his new business.

"The boys will be pleased, I can tell you."

"I will do all I can to give them satisfaction," said Philip modestly.

"Oh, you will! there's no doubt about that. How much did you pay for your fiddle?"

"I believe it cost twenty-five dollars. My father gave it to me."

"Sho! I didn't think fiddles cost so much."

"Some cost a great deal more."

"Seems a good deal to lay out, but you'll get your money back, if you can get enough to do."

"I hope so."

"Well, you must excuse me now. I've got to slick up, and go after Mary Ann Temple. She'd have been awfully disappointed if we'd had to give it up."

"Is she fond of dancing?"

"You'd better believe she is. Why, that girl could dance for four hours stiddy - without wiltin'!"

"How late do you keep it up?"

"Till eleven or twelve. You won't be sleepy, will you?"

"If I am, I will get up later to-morrow morning."

"That's all right. You can get up jest as late as you like. Lucy will save you some breakfast. We don't allow no one to go hungry here. But I must be off. You will go to the hall along with Jonas and Lucy. They'll introduce you round and see that you are taken care of." Philip congratulated himself on being so well provided for, at least for one night. The future was uncertain, but with the money which he was to receive for his services, he would be able to get along for two or three days, and he might, perhaps, if successful, obtain another similar engagement.

He had a new reason for being thankful that Squire Pope had not succeeded in depriving him of his violin, for this was likely to prove a breadwinner.

He continued to practice till it was time to go over to the hall.

CHAPTER XX.

A LIVELY EVENING.

Schoolhouse Hall, as may be inferred, was a large hall, occupying the second story of the Center Schoolhouse, and though not originally intended for dancing-parties, answered very well for that purpose.

The hall was tolerably well filled when Philip entered in company with Jonas Webb and his wife.

Philip had effaced, as well as he could, the stains of travel, had arrayed himself in a clean shirt and collar, brushed his hair neatly, and, being naturally a very good-looking boy, appeared to very good advantage, though he certainly did look young.

As he walked through the hall, with his violin under his arm, he attracted the attention of all, it having been already made known that in place of the veteran Paul Beck - a man of fifty or more - an unknown boy would furnish the music for the evening.

Philip could not avoid hearing some of the remarks which his appearance excited. "What! that little runt play the fiddle?" said one countrified young man, in a short-waisted blue coat, and tow-colored hair, plastered down on either side of his head with tallow.

"I don't believe he can play any more than I can."

"I hope he can," retained his partner - a plump, red-cheeked, young farmer's daughter. "He's very good-looking, anyhow."

"He isn't anything to brag of," said her partner jealously.

"Oh, how can you say so, Jedidiah. I See what beautiful black hair and eyes he's got, and such a lovely color on his cheeks!"

Now, Jedidiah, in appearance, was just the reverse of Philip. His hair, as already stated, was tow-color, his face was tanned, and the color rather resembled brick-dust than the deep red of our hero's cheeks.

His partner was a rustic flirt, and he was disposed to be jealous, not being certain how far she favored him. He, therefore, took offense at his partner's admiration of the young fiddler.

"He looks very common to me," said Jedidiah pettishly. "You've got a strange taste, Maria."

"Perhaps I have, and perhaps I haven't," retorted Maria, tossing her head.

"Perhaps you're in love with him?" continued Jedidiah, in a tone meant to be sarcastic,

"I should be if he was a little older," said the young lady, rather enjoying her lover's displeasure.

"I don't believe he can play at all," growled Jedidiah.

"He's fooled Abner Webb, like as not. It's a pity we couldn't have Paul Beck."

"Very likely he can play better than Paul Beck," said Maria - not because she thought so, but because she knew it would tease her partner.

"Don't be a fool, Maria," said Jedidiah, scarcely conscious of the impoliteness of his speech.

The young lady, however, resented it at once.

"I am sure you are very polite, Mr. Jedidiah Burbank - so polite that I think you had better find another partner!"

"Excuse me, Maria," said Jedidiah hastily, alarmed at the prospect of being left without a partner. "Of course, I didn't mean anything."

"If you didn't mean it, what made you say it?" retorted Maria, tossing her head. "I ain't used to being called a fool. I never knew a gentleman to make such a remark to a lady. I think you'd better find some other partner."

"I take it all back," said Jedidiah, in alarm. "I was only in fun."

"I don't like that kind of fun," said Maria, in a tone of dignified coldness.

"Then I won't joke you again. I guess he can play well enough, if Abner says so."

Miss Maria Snodgrass allowed herself to be propitiated, more especially as she herself might have been left without a partner, had she adhered to her determination and sent Jedidiah adrift.

He took his place in a quadrille, not exactly wishing Philip to fail, but rather hoping that he would prove a poor performer, in order that he might have a little triumph over Maria, who had the bad taste to prefer the young musician's appearance to his.

Meanwhile Philip, following Jonas Webb across the room, had been introduced to Frank Ingalls, who acted as manager.

"I am glad to see you, Mr. Gray," said Ingalls. "I hope we sha'n't make you work too hard. We are very fond of dancing here."

"I don't get tired very easily," answered Philip. "I hope you will be satisfied with my playing."

"No fear of that, Mr. Ingalls, I've heerd him play at home, and I tell you he can do it."

"Thank you, Mr. Webb," said Philip, bowing his acknowledgment of the compliment.

"I guess we may as well commence, Mr. Gray," said Mr. Ingalls. "The boys seem to be getting impatient. Here's the order of dances for the evening."

"Very well, Mr. Ingalls."

The manager raised his voice, and said, "Gentlemen and ladies, you already know that Beck is sick, and cannot be with us this evening, as he engaged to do. In his place we have engaged a young musician, who has already gained a great reputation in his profession -"

Philip was rather surprised to hear this, but it was not for him to gainsay it.

"Let me introduce to you Mr. Philip Gray."

Philip bowed and smiled, and, putting his violin in position, immediately commenced a lively air.

In less than five minutes the manager felt perfectly at ease concerning the young musician. It was clear that Philip understood his business. Philip himself entered into the spirit of his performance. His cheek flushed, his eyes sparkled, and he almost outdid himself.

When the first dance was concluded, there was a murmur of approval throughout the ballroom. The dancers were both surprised and pleased.

"He's a smart boy!" said more than one. "He plays as well as Paul Beck, and Paul's been play-in' for more'n twenty years."

"As well? I never heard Paul Beck play as well as that," said another.

Among those who were most pleased was Miss Maria Snodgrass.

"What do you think now, Mr. Burbank?" she said, addressing her partner. "Do you think the boy can play now?"

"Yes, he can play most as well as Paul Beck," admitted Jedidiah.

"Most as well? Paul Beck can't begin to play as well as him," returned Maria, who was not educated, and occasionally made slips in grammar.

"Just as you say, Maria," answered Jedidiah, submissively; "only don't call me Mr. Burbank."

"Why? Ain't that your name?" asked the young lady demurely.

"Not to you, Maria."

"Well, I won't, if you'll take me up and introduce me to Mr. Gray."

"What for?" asked Jedidiah jealously.

"Because I want to know him."

Mr. Burbank was obliged to obey the request of his partner.

"Oh, Mr. Gray, you play just lovely!" said Miss Snodgrass rapturously.

"Thank you for the compliment," said Philip, with a low bow.

"I like your playing ever so much better than Paul Beck's."

"You are too kind," said Philip, with another bow.

"Isn't he just lovely, Jedidiah!" said Maria, as she walked away with her lover.

"Maybe he is - I ain't a judge!" said Mr. Burbank, not very enthusiastically.

So the evening passed. Philip continued to win the favorable opinion of the merry party by his animated style of playing.

When at half-past eleven the last dance was announced, he was glad, for after his long walk, and the efforts of the evening, he felt tired.

At the conclusion, Mr. Ingalls handed him three dollars, saying:

"Here's your money, Mr. Gray, and we are much obliged to you besides."

"Thank you!" said our hero, carelessly slipping the money into his vest pocket.

The manager little imagined that it constituted his entire capital.

"I hope we may have you here again some time, Mr. Gray," continued the manager.

"Perhaps so," said Philip; "but I am not sure when I shall come this way again."

"Good night, Mr. Gray," said Miss Snodgrass effusively. "I should be glad to have you call at our house."

Philip bowed his thanks. He did not notice the dark cloud on the brow of the young lady's escort.

CHAPTER XXI.

FORTUNE SMILES AGAIN.

Notwithstanding his exertions during the day and evening, Philip rose the next day at his usual hour, and was in time for the family breakfast, at seven o'clock.

"Don't you feel tired, Mr. Gray?" asked Mrs. Webb.

"No, thank you. I slept well, and feel quite refreshed."

"He's used to it, Lucy," remarked her husband.

"They look upon me as a professional player," thought Philip.

"I think you and I ought to be more tired, for we were dancing all the evening," continued the farmer.

When they rose from the table, Philip looked for his hat.

"You're not going to leave us so soon, Mr. Gray?" said Mrs. Webb hospitably. "We shall be glad to have you stay with us a day or two, if you can content yourself."

"That's right, Lucy. I'm glad you thought to ask him," said her husband.

Philip was tempted to accept this kind invitation. He would have free board, and be at no expense, instead of spending the small sum he had earned the evening previous; but he reflected that he would be no nearer solving the problem of how he was to maintain himself, and while this was in uncertainty, he was naturally anxious.

"I am very much obliged to you both," he said. "If I come this way again, I shall be glad to call upon you, but now I think I must be pushing on."

"You'll always be welcome, Mr. Gray," said Mrs. Webb.

Philip thanked her, and soon after set out on his way.

He was more cheerful and hopeful than the day before, for then he was well nigh penniless, and now he had three dollars in his pocket.

Three dollars was not a very large sum, to be sure, but to one who had been so near destitution as Philip it seemed very important.

Besides, he had discovered in his violin a source of income, whereas, hitherto, he had looked upon it merely as a source of amusement. This made him feel more independent and self-reliant.

He had walked perhaps two miles, when he heard the rattle of wheels behind him. He did not turn his head, for there was nothing strange in this sound upon a frequented road. He did turn his head, however, when he heard a strong voice calling "Hello!"

Turning, he saw that a young man who was driving had slackened the speed of his horse, and was looking toward him.

Philip halted, and regarded the driver inquiringly.

"You're the young chap that played for a dance last night, ain't you!" said the newcomer.

"Yes, sir."

"Then you're the one I want to see - jump in, and we'll talk as we are going along."

Philip had no objection to a ride, and he accepted the invitation with alacrity. The driver, he noticed, was a young man, of pleasant manners, though dressed in a coarse suit.

"I drove over to Jonas Webb's to see you, and they told me you had just gone," he continued. "I thought maybe you'd get up late, but you was up on time. Are you engaged for this evening?"

Philip began to prick up his ears and become interested. Was it possible that his good luck was to continue, and that he was to have an opportunity of earning some more money through his faithful friend, the violin? He didn't think it well to exhibit the satisfaction he felt, and answered, in a matter-of-fact tone;

"No, I have no engagement for this evening."

"I'm glad of it," responded the young man, evidently well pleased. "You see, we had arranged to have a dance over to our place, but Mr. Beck, being sick, we thought we'd have to give it up. One of my neighbors was over last evening and heard you play, and he thought maybe we could secure you."

"I shall be glad to play for you," said Philip politely.

"What are your terms?" asked his companion.

"Three dollars and board and lodging for the time I need to stay."

"That's satisfactory. I'll engage you."

"Is it near here?" asked Philip.

"It's in Conway - only four miles from here. I'll take you right over now, and you shall stay at my house."

"Thank you, I shall find that very agreeable," said Philip.

"Does Mr. Beck live near you?" asked our hero, a little later.

"Bless you! he lives in our place."

"I suppose his services are in demand?"

"Yes, he is sent for to all the towns around. Fact is, there isn't anybody but he that can play to suit; but I expect, from what I've heard, that you can come up to him."

"I couldn't expect to do that," said Philip modestly. "I am very young yet."

"Folks do say you beat Paul. It seems wonderful, too, considering how young you are. What might be your age, now?"

"Just sixteen."

"Sho! you don't say so? Why, Paul Beck's over fifty."

"Mr. Beck won't think I'm interfering with him, will he?" asked Philip.

"Of course, he can't. We'd a had him if he was well. We can't be expected to put off the party because he's sick. That wouldn't be reasonable, now, would it?"

"I should think not."

Just then Philip became sensible that a light wagon was approaching, driven by a young lady.

He did not, however, suppose it was any one he knew till the carriage stopped, and he heard a voice saying:

"Good morning, Mr. Gray!"

Then he discovered that it was the same young lady who had asked for an introduction to him the evening previous.

"Good morning, Miss Snodgrass!" he said politely, remembering, fortunately, the young lady's name.

Meanwhile, Maria and Philip's drivers had also exchanged salutations, for they were acquainted.

"And where are you carrying Mr. Gray, Mr. Blake?"

she asked.

"I'm carrying him over to our place. He's going to play for us this evening."

"Is there going to be a dance in Conway this evening?" inquired Miss Snodgrass, with sudden interest.

"Yes. Won't you come over?"

"I will, if I can get Jedidiah to bring me," answered Maria.

"I guess there's no doubt about that," answered Andrew Blake, who knew very well Jedidiah's devotion to the young lady.

"Oh, I don't know!" answered Maria coquet-tishly. "Perhaps he won't care for my company."

"If he doesn't, you won't have any trouble in finding another beau."

After a little more conversation, the young lady drove away; but not without expressing to Philip her delight at having another chance to hear his beautiful playing.

"She'll be there," said Andrew Blake, as they drove away. "She makes Jedidiah Burbank do just as she orders him."

"Are they engaged?" asked our hero.

"Yes, I expect so; but there may be some chance of your cutting him out, if you try. The young lady seems to admire you."

Philip smiled.

"I am only a boy of sixteen," he said. "I am too young to think of such things. I won't interfere with Mr. Burbank."

"Jedidiah's apt to be jealous," said Blake, "and Maria likes to torment him. However, she'll end by marrying him, I guess."

In half an hour or thereabouts, Andrew Blake drew up at the gate of a small but neat house on the main street in Conway. He was a carpenter, as Philip afterward found, and had built the house himself. He was probably of about the same age as Jonas Webb, and like him was married to a young wife.

During the afternoon, Philip, being left pretty much to his own devices, took a walk in and about the village, ascending a hill at one side, which afforded him a fine view of that and neighboring villages.

He was pleasantly received and hospitably entertained at the house of Mr. Blake, and about quarter of eight started out for the hall, at which he was to play, in company with his host and hostess.

As they approached the hall, a young man approached them with a perplexed face.

"What do you think, Andrew?" he said. "Paul Beck's in the hall, as mad as a hatter, and he vows he'll play himself. He says he was engaged, and no one shall take his place."

Andrew Blake looked disturbed, and Philip shared in his feeling. Was he to lose his engagement, after all?

CHAPTER XXII.

RIVAL MUSICIANS.

They entered the hall, which was already well filled, for the young people of both sexes liked to have as long a time for enjoyment as possible.

At the head of the hall, in the center of a group, stood a tall, thin man, dressed in solemn black, with a violin under his arm. His face, which looked like that of a sick man, was marked by an angry expression, and this, indeed, was his feeling.

"I suppose that's Mr. Beck?" said Philip.

"Yes, it is," answered Andrew Blake, in evident discomposure. "What on earth brings him here from a sick-bed, I can't understand. I heard that he had a fever."

The fact was that Paul Beck was jealous of his reputation as a musician. It was satisfactory to him to think that he was so indispensable that no one could take his place. He had sent word to the committee that he should be unable to play for them, supposing, of course, that they would be compelled to give up the party. When intelligence was brought to him during the afternoon that it would come off, and that another musician had been engaged in his place, he was not only disturbed, but angry, though, of course, the latter feeling was wholly unreasonable. He determined that he would be present, at any rate, no matter how unfit his sickness rendered him for the evening's work. He resolved to have no rival, and to permit no one to take his place in his own town.

It did not seem to occur to Mr. Beck that, having formally declined the engagement on account of sickness, he had no claim whatever on the committee, and was, in fact, an interloper. It was in vain that his sister protested against his imprudence. (He was an old bachelor and his sister kept house for him.) He insisted on dressing himself and making his way to the hall, where, as was to be expected, his arrival produced considerable embarrassment.

Paul Beck stood in sullen impatience awaiting the arrival of his rival.

It so happened that no one had thought to mention to him that it was a boy. He was prepared to see a full-grown man.

Philip followed Andrew Blake up to the central group.

"Who is it, I say," Mr. Beck was inquiring, "that engaged another musician to take my place?"

"No one, sir," answered Andrew Blake firmly, for Mr. Beck's unreasonableness provoked him. "I engaged a musician to play this evening, but it was not in your place, for you had sent us word that you could not appear."

"Where is he, I say?" continued Paul Beck sourly.

"Here he is," replied Blake, drawing toward our hero, who felt that he was placed in an awkward position.

"Why, he's only a baby!" said Beck, surveying our hero contemptuously.

Philip's cheek flushed, and he, too, began to feel angry.

"He isn't as old as you are, Mr. Beck," said Andrew Blake manfully, "but you'll find he understands his business."

"I certainly didn't expect you to get a child in my place," said Paul Beck scornfully.

"I suppose a musicain may know how to play, if he isn't sixty-five," said Miss Maria Snod-grass, who had listened indignantly to Mr. Beck's contemptuous remarks about our hero, whose cause she so enthusiastically championed.

Poor Mr. Beck! He was sensitive about his age, and nothing could have cut him more cruelly than this exaggeration of it. He was really fifty-five, and looked at least sixty, but he fondly flattered himself that he looked under fifty. "Sixty-five!" he repeated furiously. "Who says I am sixty-five?"

"Well, you look about that age," said Maria, with malicious pleasure.

"I shall have to live a good many years before I am sixty," said Paul Beck angrily. "But that's either here nor there. You engaged me to play to-night, and I am ready to do it."

Andrew Blake felt the difficulty of his position, but he did not mean to desert the boy-musician whom he had engaged.

"Mr. Beck," said he, "we shall be glad to have you serve us on another occasion, but to-night Mr. Gray, here, is engaged. You gave up the engagement of your own accord, and that ended the matter, so far as you are concerned."

"Do you refuse to let me play?" demanded Paul Beck, his pale cheek glowing with anger and mortification.

"You understand why," answered Blake. "This young man is engaged, and we have no right to break the engagement."

Philip, who had felt the embarrassment of his position, had meanwhile made up his mind what to do. The three dollars he expected to earn were important to him, but he didn't care to make trouble. He did not doubt that his lodging and meals would be given him, and that would be something. Accordingly, he spoke:

"I have been engaged, it is true," he said, "but if Mr. Beck wants to play I will resign my engagement and stay and hear him."

"No, no!" exclaimed several - Mr. Blake and Miss Snodgrass being among them.

"Mr. Gray, you were regularly engaged," said one of the committee.

"That's true," answered Philip, "and," he couldn't help adding, "I should be justified in insisting upon playing; but since Mr. Beck seems to feel so bad about it, I will give way to him."

He spoke manfully, and there was no sign of weakness or submission about him. He asserted his rights, while he expressed his willingness to surrender them.

There was a little consultation among the committee. They were all disgusted with the conduct of Paul Beck, and were unwilling that he should triumph. At the same time, as they might need his services at some future time, they did not wish wholly to alienate him.

Finally, they announced their decision through Andrew Blake.

"We are not willing to accept Mr. Gray's resignation wholly," he said, "but we propose that he and Mr. Beck shall divide the evening's work between them - each to receive half the usual compensation."

There was considerable applause, for it seemed to be a suitable compromise, and would enable the company to compare the merits of the rival musicians.

"I agree," said Philip promptly.

"What do you say, Mr. Beck?" asked Andrew Blake.

Now, while Paul Beck did not like to give up half the honor, he felt thoroughly convinced that Philip was only a beginner, and that he, as an experienced player, could easily eclipse him, and thus gain a triumph which would be very gratifying to his pride.

As for the compensation, to do him justice, he did not much care for that, being a man of very good means. He played more for glory than for pay - though he, of course, had no objection to receiving compensation.

"I have no objections," he said. "If you want to give the boy a chance to practice a little, I am willing."

Philip understood the sneer, and he secretly determined to do his best.

The committee was much pleased at the satisfactory conclusion of what had threatened to be a very troublesome dispute, and it was arranged, Philip consenting, that Mr. Beck should play first.

The old musician played, in a confident manner, a familiar dancing-tune, accompanying his playing with various contortions of the face and twistings of his figure, supposed to express feeling. It was a fair performance, but mechanical, and did not indicate anything but very ordinary talent. His time was good, and dancers always found his playing satisfactory.

When Paul Beck had completed his task, he looked about him complacently, as if to say, "Let the boy beat that if he can," and sat down.

Philip had listened to Mr. Beck with attention. He was anxious to learn how powerful a rival he had to compete with. What he heard did not alarm him, but rather gave him confidence.

CHAPTER XXIII.

AN HOUR OF TRIUMPH.

When Paul rose and stood before this audience, violin in hand, he certainly presented quite a strong contrast to his rival.

Paul Beck, as we have already said, was a tall, thin, lantern-jawed man, clad in solemn black, his face of a sickly, sallow hue.

Philip was of fair height, for his age, with a bright, expressive face, his hair of a chestnut shade, and looking the very picture of boyish health. His very appearance made a pleasant impression upon those present.

"He's a nice-looking boy," thought more than one, "but he looks too young to know much about the violin."

But when Philip began to play, there was general surprise. In a dancing-tune there was not much chance for the exhibition of talent, but his delicate touch and evident perfect mastery of his instrument were immediately apparent. In comparison, the playing of Paul Beck seemed wooden and mechanical.

There was a murmur of approbation, and when Philip

had finished his first part of the program, he was saluted by hearty applause, which he acknowledged by a modest and graceful bow.

Paul Beck's face, as his young rival proceeded in his playing, was an interesting study. He was very disagreeably surprised. He had made up his mind that Philip could not play at all, or, at any rate, would prove to be a mere tyro and bungler, and he could hardly believe his ears when he heard the sounds which Philip evoked from his violin.

In spite of his self-conceit, he secretly acknowledged that Philip even now was his superior, and in time would leave him so far behind that there could be no comparison between them.

It was not a pleasant discovery for a man who had prided himself for many years on his superiority as a musician. If it had been a man of established fame it would have been different, but to be compelled to yield the palm to an unknown boy, was certainly mortifying.

When he heard the applause that followed Philip's performance, and remembered that none had been called forth by his own, he determined that he would not play again that evening. He did not like to risk the comparison which he was sure would be made between himself and Philip. So, when Andrew Blake came up to him and asked him to play for the next dance, he shook his head. "I don't feel well enough," he said "I thought I was stronger than I am."

"Do you want the boy to play all the rest of the evening?"

"Yes; he plays very fairly," said Beck, in a patronizing manner, which implied his own superiority.

"There can be no doubt about that," said Andrew Blake, with emphasis, for he understood Mr. Beck's meaning, and resented it as one of the warmest admirers of the boy-musician whom he had engaged.

But Paul Beck would not for the world have revealed his real opinion of Philip's merits.

"Yes," he continued, "he plays better than I expected. I guess you can get along with him."

"How shall we arrange about the compensation, Mr. Beck?" asked Blake. "We ought in that case to give him more than half."

"Oh, you can give him the whole," answered Beck carelessly. "If I felt well enough to play, I would do my part, but I think it will be better for me to go home and go to bed."

His decision was communicated to Philip, who felt impelled by politeness to express his regrets to Mr. Beck.

"I am sorry you don't feel able to play, Mr. Beck," he said politely.

"Oh, it's of no consequence, as they've got some one to take my place," returned Beck coldly.

"I should be glad to hear you play again," continued Philip.

Paul Beck nodded slightly, but he felt too much mortified to reciprocate Philip's friendly advances. Half an hour later he left the hall.

The dancers by no means regretted the change of arrangement. They evidently preferred the young musician to his elderly rival. The only one to express regret was Miss Maria Snodgrass.

"I declare it's a shame Mr. Beck has given up," she said. "I wanted you to dance with me, Mr. Gray. I am sure if you can dance as well as you can play, you would get along perfectly lovely. Now you've got to play, and can't dance at all."

"It isn't leap-year, Maria," said Jedidiah Burbank, in a jealous tone.

Miss Snodgrass turned upon him angrily:

"You needn't put in your oar, Jedidiah Burbank!" she said. "I guess I know what I'm about. If it was leap-year fifty times over, I wouldn't offer myself to you!"

And the young lady tossed her head in a very decided manner.

"Now don't get mad, Maria!" implored Jedidiah, feeling that at the prompting of jealousy; he had put his foot in it. "I didn't mean nothing."

"Then you'd better say nothing next time," retorted the young lady.

Meanwhile, Philip acknowledged the young lady's politeness by a smile and a bow, assuring her that if it had been possible, it would have given him great pleasure to dance with her.

"If Mr. Burbank will play for me," he said with a glance at the young man, "I shall be glad to dance."

Miss Snodgrass burst out laughing.

"Jedidiah couldn't play well enough for an old cow to dance by," she said.

"There ain't any old cows here," said Jedidiah, vexed at being ridiculed.

"Well, there are some calves, anyway," retorted Maria, laughing heartily.

Poor Jedidiah! It is to be feared that he will have a hard time when he becomes the husband of the fair Maria. She will undoubtedly be the head of the new matrimonial firm.

There was nothing further to mar the harmony of the evening. It had begun with indications of a storm, but the clouds had vanished, and when Mr. Beck left the hall, there was nothing left to disturb the enjoyment of those present.

The favorable opinions expressed when Philip commenced playing were repeated again and again, as the evening slipped away.

"I tell you, he's a regular genius!" one enthusiastic admirer said to his companion. "Paul Beck can't hold a candle to him."

"That's so. He's smart, and no mistake."

Poor Mr. Beck! It was fortunate he was unable to hear these comparisons made. He could not brook a rival near the throne, and had gone home in low spirits, feeling that he could never again hold his head as high as he had done.

When the dancing was over, there was a brief conference of the committee of management, the subject of which was soon made known.

Andrew Blake approached Philip and said:

"Mr. Gray, some of us would like to hear you play something else, if you are not tired - not a dancing-tune."

"I shall be very happy to comply with your request," answered Philip.

He spoke sincerely, for he saw that all were pleased with him, and it is gratifying to be appreciated.

He paused a moment in thought, and then began to play the "Carnival of Venice," with variations. It had been taught him by his father, and he had played it so often that his execution was all that could be desired. The variations were of a showy and popular character, and very well adapted to impress an audience like that to which he was playing.

"Beautiful! Beautiful!" exclaimed the young ladies, while their partners pronounced it "tip-top" and "first-rate," by which they probably meant very much the same thing.

"Oh, Mr. Gray!" exclaimed Miss Snodgrass fervently. "You play like a seraphim!"

"Thank you!" said Philip, smiling. "I never heard a seraphim play on the violin, but I am sure your remark is very complimentary."

"I wish you could play like that, Jedidiah," said Maria.

"I'll learn to play, if you want me to," said Mr. Burbank.

"Thank you! You're very obliging," said Maria; "but I won't trouble you. You haven't got a genius for it, like Mr. Gray."

The evening was over at length, and again Philip was made the happy recipient of three dollars. His first week had certainly been unexpectedly prosperous.

"This is better than staying in the Norton Poorhouse!" he said to himself.

Horatio Alger

CHAPTER XXIV.

LORENZO RICCABOCCA.

Philip's reputation as a musician was materially increased by his second night's performance. To adopt a military term, he had crossed swords with the veteran fiddler, Paul Beck, and, in the opinion of all who heard both, had far surpassed him.

This was said openly to Philip by more than one; but he was modest, and had too much tact and good taste to openly agree with them. This modesty raised him higher in the opinion of his admirers.

He was invited by the Blakes to prolong his visit, but preferred to continue on his journey - though his plans were, necessarily, not clearly defined.

Andrew Blake carried him five miles on his way, and from that point our hero used the means of locomotion with which nature had supplied him.

Some six miles farther on there was a manufacturing town of considerable size, named Wilkesville, and it occurred to him that this would be a good place at which to pass the night.

Something might turn up for him there. He hardly

knew what, but the two unexpected strokes of luck which he had had thus far encouraged him to think that a third might come to him.

Philip continued on his way - his small pack of clothing in one hand and his violin under his arm. Being in no especial hurry - for it was only the middle of the forenoon - he bethought himself to sit down and rest at the first convenient and inviting place.

He soon came to a large elm tree, which, with its spreading branches, offered a pleasant and grateful shade.

He threw himself down and lay back on the greensward, in pleasant contemplation, when he heard a gentle cough - as of one who wished to attract attention. Looking up he observed close at hand, a tall man, dressed in black, with long hair, which fell over his shirt collar and shoulders.

He wore a broad collar and black satin necktie, and his hair was parted in the middle. His appearance was certainly peculiar, and excited our hero's curiosity.

"My young friend," he said, "you have chosen a pleasant resting-place beneath this umbrageous monarch of the grove." "Yes, sir," answered Philip, wondering whether the stranger was a poet.

"May I also recline beneath it?" asked the newcomer.

"Certainly, sir. It is large enough to shelter us both."

"Quite true; but I did not wish to intrude upon your meditations."

"My meditations are not of much account," answered Philip, laughing.

"I see you are modest. Am I right in supposing that yonder case contains a violin?"

"Yes, sir."

"Then you are a musician?"

"A little of one," replied Philip.

"May I ask - excuse my curiosity - if you play professionally?"

"Perhaps he may help me to an engagement," thought our hero, and he said readily, "I do."

"Indeed!" said the stranger, appearing pleased. "What style of music do you play?"

"For each of the last two evenings I have played for dancing-parties."

"Alone?"

"Yes."

"You do not confine yourself to dancing-music?"

"Oh, no! I prefer other kinds; but dancing-tunes seem most in demand, and I have my living to make." The stranger seemed still more gratified.

"I am delighted to have met you, Mr. - Ahem!" he paused, and looked inquiringly at Philip.

"Gray."

"Mr. Gray, I believe Providence has brought us together. I see you are surprised."

Philip certainly did look puzzled, as he well might.

"I must explain myself more clearly. I am Professor Lorenzo Riccabocca, the famous elocutionist and dramatic reader."

Philip bowed.

"Doubtless you have heard of me?" said the professor inquiringly.

"I have never lived in large places," answered Philip, in some embarrassment, "or no doubt your name would be familiar to me."

"To be sure, that must make a difference. For years," said the professor, "I have given dramatic readings to crowded houses, and everywhere my merits have been conceded by the educated and refined."

Philip could not help wondering how it happened in that case that the professor should look so seedy. A genius appreciated so highly ought to have brought in more gold and silver.

Perhaps Professor Riccabocca understood Philip's expressive look, for he went to to say:

"The public has repaid me richly for the exercise of my talent; but, alas, my young friend, I must confess that I have no head for business. I invested my savings unwisely, and ascertained a month since that I had lost all."

"That was a great pity!" said Philip sympathizingly.

"It was, indeed! It quite unmanned me!" said the professor, wiping away a tear. "I felt that all ambition was quite gone, and I was mad and sick. Indeed, only a week since I rose from a sick-bed. But Lorenzo is himself again!" he exclaimed, striking his breast energetically. "I will not succumb to Fate. I will again court the favor of the public, and this time I will take care of the ducats my admirers bestow upon me."

"I should think that was a good plan," said Philip.

"I will begin at once. Nearby is a town devoted to the mammon of trade, yet among its busy thousands there must be many that will appreciate the genius of Lorenzo Riccabocca."

"I hope so," answered Philip politely.

He could not help thinking that the professor was rather self-conceited, and he hardly thought it in good taste for him to refer so boastfully to his genius.

"I wish you, Mr. Gray, to assist me in my project," continued the professor.

"How can I do so, sir?" inquired Philip.

"Let me tell you. I propose that we enter into a professional partnership, that we give an entertainment partly musical, partly dramatic. I will draw up a program, including some of my most humorous recitations and impersonations, while interspersed among them will be musical selections contributed by yourself. Do you comprehend?"

"Yes," answered Philip, nodding.

"And what do you think of it?"

"I think well of it," replied the boy-musician.

He did think well of it. It might not draw a large audience, this mixed entertainment, but it would surely pay something; and it would interfere with no plans of his own, for, in truth, he had none.

"Then you will cooperate with me?" said the professor.

"Yes, professor."

"Give me your hand!" exclaimed Riccabocca dramatically. "Mr. Gray, it is a perfect bonanza of an idea. I may tell you, in confidence, I was always a genius for ideas. Might I ask a favor of you?"

"Certainly, sir."

"Give me a touch of your quality. Let me hear you play."

Philip drew his violin from its case and played for his new professional partner "The Carnival of Venice," with variations - the same which had been received with so much favor the evening previous.

Professor Riccabocca listened attentively, and was evidently agreeably surprised. He was not a musician, but he saw that Philip was a much better player than he had anticipated, and this, of course, was likely to improve their chances of pecuniary success.

"You are a splendid performer," he said enthusiastically. "You shall come out under my auspices and win fame. I predict for you a professional triumph."

"Thank you," said Philip, gratified by this tribute from a man of worldly experience. "I hope you will prove a true prophet."

"And now, Mr. Gray, let us proceed on our way. We must get lodgings in Wilkesville, and make arrangements for our entertainment. I feel new courage, now that I have obtained so able a partner. Wilkesville little knows what is in store for her. We shall go, see, and conquer!"

An hour later Philip and his new partner entered Wilkesville.

CHAPTER XXV.

A CHANGE OF NAME.

Wilkesville was an inland city, of from fifteen to twenty thousand inhabitants.

As Philip and the professor passed along the principal street, they saw various stores of different kinds, with here and there a large, high, plain-looking structure, which they were told was used for the manufacture of shoes.

"Wilkesville will give us a large audience," he said, in a tone of satisfaction.

"I hope so," said our hero.

"Hope so? I know so!" said the professor confidently. "The town is full of young men, employed in shoe-making. They are fond of amusement, and they will gladly seize an opportunity of patronizing a first-class entertainment like ours."

The professor's reasoning seemed good, but logic sometimes fails, and Philip was not quite so sanguine. He said nothing, however, to dampen the ardor of his partner.

"Let me see," said the professor, pausing, "yonder stands the Wilkesville Hotel. We had better put up there."

It was a brick structure of considerable size, and seemed to have some pretensions to fashion.

"Do you know how much they charge?" asked Philip prudently.

"No; I neither know nor care," answered Professor Riccabocca loftily.

"But," said Philip, "I haven't much money."

"Nor I," admitted Riccabocca. "But it is absolutely necessary for us to stop at a first-class place. We must not let the citizens suppose that we are tramps or vagabonds. They will judge us by our surroundings."

"There is something in that," said Philip. "But suppose we don't succeed!"

"Succeed? We must succeed!" said the professor, striking an attitude. "In the vocabulary of youth, there's no such word as 'fail'! Away with timid caution! Our watchword be success!"

"Of course, you have much more experience than I," said Philip.

"Certainly I have! We must keep up appearances. Be guided by me, and all will come right."

Philip reflected that they could not very well make less than their expenses, and accordingly he acceded to the professor's plans. They entered the hotel, and Professor Riccabocca, assuming a dignified, important step, walked up to the office. "Sir," said he, to the clerk, "my companion and myself would like an apartment, one eligibly located, and of ample size."

"You can be accommodated, sir," answered the young man politely. "Will you enter your names?"

Opening the hotel register, the elocutionist, with various flourishes, entered, this name: "Professor Lorenzo Riccabocca, Elocutionist and Dramatic Reader."

"Shall I enter your name?" he asked of Philip.

"If you please."

This was the way Professor Riccabocca complied with his request: "Philip de Gray, the Wonderful Boy-musician."

He turned the book, so that the clerk could see the entries.

"We propose to give an entertainment in Wilkesville," he said.

"I am glad to hear it," said the clerk politely.

"After dinner I will consult you as to what steps to take. Is there anything in the way of amusement going on in town this evening?"

"Yes, there is a concert, chiefly of home-talent, in Music Hall. There is nothing announced for to-morrow evening."

"Then we will fix upon to-morrow evening. It will give us more time to get out hand-bills, etc. Is there a printing-office in town?"

"Oh, yes, sir. We have a daily paper."

"Is the office near at hand?"

"Yes, sir. It is on the corner of the next street."

"That will do for the present. We will go up to our apartment. Will dinner be ready soon?"

"In half an hour."

Here the servant made his appearance, and the professor, with a wave of his hand, said:

"Lead on, Mr. de Gray! I will follow."

CHAPTER XXVI.

A PROMISING PLAN.

They were shown into a front room, of good size, containing two beds. The servant handed them the key, and left them.

"This looks very comfortable, Mr. de Gray," said the professor, rubbing his hands with satisfaction.

"Why do you call me Mr. de Gray?" asked Philip, thinking he had been misunderstood. "It is plain Gray, without any de."

"I am only using your professional name," answered the professor. "Don't you know people will think a great deal more of you if they suppose you to be a foreigner?"

Philip laughed.

"Is Lorenzo Riccabocca your true or professional name, professor?" he asked.

"Professional, of course. My real name - I impart it to you in the strictest confidence - is Lemuel Jones. Think of it. How would that look on a poster?"

"It would not be so impressive as the other."

"Of course not; and the public need to be impressed. I thank thee for that word, Mr. de Gray. By the way, it's rather a pity I didn't give you a Spanish or Italian name."

"But I can't speak either language. It would be seen through at once."

"People wouldn't think of asking. You'd be safe enough. They will generally swallow all you choose to say."

They went down to dinner presently, and the professor - Philip could not help thinking - ate as if he were half-starved. He explained afterward that elocutionary effort taxes the strength severely, and makes hearty eating a necessity.

After dinner was over the professor said:

"Are you content, Mr. de Gray, to leave me to make the necessary arrangements?"

"I should prefer that you would," said Philip, and he spoke sincerely. "Probably you understand much better than I what needs to be done."

"'Tis well! Your confidence is well placed," said the professor, with a wave of his hand. "Shall you remain in the hotel?"

"No, I think I will walk about the town and see a little of it. I have never been here before."

Philip took a walk through the principal streets, surveying with curiosity the principal building's, for, though there was nothing particularly remarkable about them, he was a young traveler, to whom everything was new. He could not help thinking of his late home, and in particular of Frank Dunbar, his special friend, and he resolved during the afternoon to write a letter to Frank, apprising him of his luck thus far. He knew that Frank would feel anxious about him, and would be delighted to hear of his success as a musician.

He went into a book-store and bought a sheet of paper and an envelope.

He had just completed his letter, when his partner entered the reading-room of the hotel with a brisk step.

"Mr. de Gray," he said, "I have made all necessary arrangements. I have hired the hall for to-morrow evening - five dollars - ordered some tickets and posters at the printing-office, and secured a first-class notice in to-morrow morning's paper. Everybody in Wilkesville will know before to-morrow night that they will have the opportunity of attending a first-class performance at the Music Hall."

"It seems to me the necessary expenses are considerable," said Philip uneasily.

"Of course they are; but what does that matter?"

"What is to be the price of tickets?"

"General admission, twenty-five cents; reserved seats, fifty cents, and children under twelve, fifteen cents.

How does that strike you!"

"Will anyone be willing to pay fifty cents to hear us?" asked Philip.

"Fifty cents! It will be richly worth a dollar!" said the professor loftily.

"I suppose he knows best," thought Philip. "I hope all will come out right. If it does we can try the combination in other places."

CHAPTER XXVII.

UNEXPECTED HONORS.

The next morning at breakfast, Professor Riccabocca handed Philip a copy of the Wilkesville Daily Bulletin. Pointing to a paragraph on the editorial page, he said, in a tone of pride and satisfaction:

"Read that, Mr. de Gray."

It ran thus:

"We congratulate the citizens of Wilkesville on the remarkable entertainment which they will have an opportunity of enjoying this evening at the Music Hall. Professor Lorenzo Riccabocca, whose fame as an elocutionist and dramatic reader has made his name a household word throughout Europe and America, will give some of his choice recitals and personations, assisted by Philip de Gray, the wonderful boy-musician, whose talent as a violin-player has been greeted with rapturous applause in all parts of the United States. It is universally acknowledged that no one of his age has ever equaled him. He, as well as Professor Riccabocca, will give but a limited series of entertainments in this country, having received flattering inducements to cross the Atlantic, and appear professionally in London, Paris, and the chief cities of the Continent. Fifty cents is the pitiful sum for which our citizens will have it put in their power to hear this wonderful combination of talent. This secures a reserved seat."

Philip read this notice with increasing amazement.

"What do you think of that, Mr. de Gray?" asked the professor gleefully. "Won't that make Wilkesville open its eyes, eh?"

"It has made me open my eyes, professor," said Philip.

"Ha, ha!" said the professor, appearing amused.

"How soon are we to sail for Europe?" asked Philip, smiling.

"When Queen Victoria sends our passage-money," answered Riccabocca, laughing.

"I see that your name is a household word in Europe. Were you ever there?"

"Never."

"Then how can that be?"

"Mr. de Gray, your performances have been greeted with applause in all parts of the United States. How do you explain that?"

"I don't pretend to explain it. I wasn't aware that my name had ever been heard of a hundred miles from here."

"It has not, but it will be. I have only been predicting a little. The paragraph isn't true now, but it will be some time, if we live and prosper."

"But I don't like to be looked upon as a humbug, professor," said Philip uneasily.

"You won't be. You are really a fine player, or I wouldn't consent to appear with you. The name of Riccabocca, Mr. de Gray, I may truthfully say, is well known. I have appeared in the leading cities of America. They were particularly enthusiastic in Chicago," he added pensively. "I wish I could find a paragraph from one of their leading papers, comparing my rendering of the soliloquy in 'Hamlet' to Edwin Booth's, rather to the disadvantage of that tragedian."

"I would like to read the notice," said Philip, who had very strong doubts as to whether such a paragraph had ever appeared in print.

"You shall see it. It will turn up somewhere. I laid it aside carefully, for I confess, Mr. de Gray, it gratified me much. I have only one thing to regret: I should myself have gone on the stage, and essayed leading tragic roles. It may not be too late now. What do you think?"

"I can tell better after I have heard you, professor," answered Philip.

"True, you can. Mr. de Gray," continued the professor, lowering his voice, "notice how much attention we are receiving from the guests at the tables. They have doubtless read the notice of our evening enter-tainment."

Philip looked round the room, which was of good size, and contained some thirty or more guests, and he saw that the professor was right.

He met several curious glances, some fair ladies expressing interest as well as curiosity, and his face flushed.

"Gratifying, isn't it?" said the professor, smiling.

"No, I don't think it is," answered our hero.

"Why not?" demanded Professor Riccabocca, appearing amazed.

"If all were true, it might be," replied Philip. "As it is, I feel like a humbug."

"Humbug pays in this world," said the professor cheerfully. "By the way, there's another little paragraph to which I will call your attention."

Philip read this additional item:

"We understand that Professor Riecabocca and Mr. Philip de Gray have received a cable despatch from the Prince of Wales, inviting them to instruct his sons in elocution and music, at a very liberal salary. They have this proposal under consideration, though they are naturally rather reluctant to give up the plaudits of the public, even for so honorable a position."

"Professor Riccabocca," said Philip, considerably annoyed by this audacious invention, "you ought to have consulted me before publishing such a falsehood as this."

"Falsehood, Mr. de Gray? Really I'm shocked! Gentlemen don't use such words, or make such charges."

"You don't mean to say it's true that we have received any such telegram?"

"No; of course not."

"Then why didn't I use the right word?"

"It's an innocent little fiction, my young friend - a fiction that will do no one any harm, but will cause us to be regarded with extraordinary interest."

Here the thought occurred to Philip that he, the future instructor of British royalty, had only just escaped from a poorhouse, and it seemed to him so droll that he burst out laughing.

"Why do you laugh, Mr. de Gray?" asked the professor, a little suspiciously.

"I was thinking of something amusing," said Philip.

"Well, well! We shall have cause to laugh when we play this evening to a crowded house."

"I hope so. But, professor, if we keep together, you mustn't print any more such paragraphs about me. Of course, I am not responsible for what you say about yourself."

"Oh, it will be all right!" said Riccabocca. "What are you going to do with yourself?"

"I shall practice a little in my room, for I want to play well to-night. When I get tired I shall take a walk."

"Very wise - very judicious. I don't need to do it, being, as I may say, a veteran reader. I wouldn't rehearse if I were to play this evening before the president and all the distinguished men of the nation."

"I don't feel so confident of myself," said Philip.

"No, of course not. By the way, can you lend me fifty cents, Mr. de Gray?"

"Certainly."

"I don't want to break a ten."

Professor Riccabocca didn't mention that the only ten he had was a ten-cent piece.

Slipping Philip's half-dollar into his vest pocket, he said carelessly:

"We'll take this into the account when we divide the proceeds of the entertainment."

"Very well," said Philip.

He went up to his room and played for an hour or more, rehearsing the different pieces he had selected for the evening, and then, feeling the need of a little fresh air, he took a walk.

In different parts of the town he saw posters, on which his name was printed in large letters.

"It seems almost like a joke!" he said to himself.

Just then he heard his name called, and, looking up, he recognized a young fellow, of sixteen or thereabouts, who had formerly lived in Norton. It seemed pleasant to see a familiar face.

"Why, Morris Lovett," he exclaimed "I didn't know you were here!"

"Yes; I'm clerk in a store. Are you the one that is going to give an entertainment tonight?"

"Yes," answered Philip, smiling.

"I didn't know you were such a great player," said Morris, regarding our hero with new respect.

He had read the morning paper.

"Nor I," said Philip, laughing.

"Are you going to Europe soon?"

"It isn't decided yet!" Philip answered, laughing.

"I wish I had your chance."

"Come and hear me this evening, at any rate," said Philip. "Call at the hotel, at six o'clock, and I'll give you a ticket."

"I'll be sure to come," said Morris, well pleased.

CHAPTER XXVIII.

A TRIUMPHANT SUCCESS.

Philip took another walk in the afternoon, and was rather amused to see how much attention he received. When he drew near the hotel he was stared at by several gaping youngsters, who apparently were stationed there for no other purpose. He overheard their whispers:

"That's him! That's Philip de Gray, the wonderful fiddler!"

"I never suspected, when I lived at Norton, that I was so much of a curiosity," he said to himself. "I wish I knew what they'll say about me to-morrow."

At six o'clock Morris Lovett called and received his ticket.

"You'll have a big house to-night, Philip," he said. "I know a lot of fellows that are going."

"I am glad to hear it," said Philip, well pleased, for he concluded that if such were the case his purse would be considerably heavier the next day.

"It's strange how quick you've come up;" said Morris.

"I never expected you'd be so famous.

"Nor I," said Philip, laughing.

"I'd give anything if I could have my name posted round like yours."

"Perhaps you will have, some time."

"Oh, no! I couldn't play more'n a pig," said Morris decidedly. "I'll have to be a clerk, and stick to business."

"You'll make more money in the end that way, Morris, even if your name isn't printed in capitals."

They retired into a small room adjoining the stage, to prepare for their appearance.

The professor rubbed his hands in glee.

"Did you see what a house we have, Mr. de Gray?"

"Yes, professor."

"I think there'll be a hundred dollars over and above expenses."

"That will be splendid!" said Philip, naturally elated.

"The firm of Riccaboeca and De Gray is starting swimmingly."

"So it is. I hope it will continue so."

"Here is the program, Mr. de Gray. You will observe

that I appear first, in my famous soliloquy. You will follow, with the 'Carnival of Venice.' Do you feel agitated?"

"Oh, no. I am so used to playing that I shall not feel at all bashful."

"That is well."

"I would like to be on the stage, professor, to hear you."

"Certainly. I have anticipated your desire, and provided an extra chair."

The time came, and Professor Riccabocca stepped upon the stage, his manner full of dignity, and advanced to the desk. Philip took a chair a little to the rear.

Their entrance was greeted by hearty applause. The professor made a stately bow, and a brief introductory speech, in which he said several things about Philip and himself which rather astonished our hero. Then he began to recite the soliloquy.

Probably it was never before so amazingly recited. Professor Riccabocca's gestures, facial contortions, and inflections were very remarkable. Philip almost suspected that he was essaying a burlesque role.

The mature portion of the audience were evidently puzzled, but the small boys were delighted, and with some of the young men, stamped vigorously at the close.

Professor Riccabocea bowed modestly, and said:

"Gentlemen and ladies, you will now have the pleasure of listening to the young and talented Philip de Gray, the wonderful boy-musician, in his unrivaled rendition of the 'Carnival of Venice.'"

Philip rose, coloring a little with shame a I this high-flown introduction, and came forward.

All applauded heartily, for sympathy is always felt for a young performer, especially when he has a manly bearing and an attractive face, such as our hero possessed.

Philip was determined to do his best. Indeed, after being advertised and announced as a boy wonder, he felt that he could not do otherwise.

He commenced, and soon lost himself in the music he loved so well, so that before he had half finished he had quite forgotten his audience, and half started at the boisterous applause which followed. He bowed his acknowledgments, but found this would not do.

He was forced to play it a second time, greatly to the apparent satisfaction of the audience. It was clear that, whatever might be thought of Professor Riccabocea's recitation, the young violinist had not disappointed his audience.

Philip could see, in a seat near the stage, the beaming face of his friend Morris Lovett, who was delighted at the success of his old acquaintance, and anticipated the reflected glory which he received, from its being known that he was a friend of the wonderful young musician.

Professor Riccabocca came forward again, and recited a poem called "The Maniac," each stanza ending with the line: "I am not mad, but soon shall be."

He stamped, raved, tore his hair, and made altogether a very grotesque appearance.

Philip could hardly forbear laughing, and some of the boys in the front seats didn't restrain themselves, Some of the older people wondered how such a man should be selected by the Prince of Wales to instruct his sons in elocution - not suspecting that the newspaper paragraph making mention of this was only a daring invention of the eminent professor.

Next came another musical selection by Philip, which was as cordially received as the first.

I do not propose to weary the reader by a recital of the program and a detailed account of each performance. It is enough to say that Professor Riccabocca excited some amusement, but was only tolerated for the sake of Philip's playing.

Naturally, our hero was better received on account of his youth, but had he been twice as old his playing would have given satisfaction and pleasure.

So passed an hour and a half, and the musical entertainment was over. Philip felt that he had reason to be satisfied. Highly as he had been heralded, no one appeared to feel disappointed by his part of the performance.

"Mr. de Gray," said the professor, when they reached the hotel, "you did splendidly. We have made a complete success."

"It is very gratifying," said Philip.

"I felt sure that the public would appreciate us. I think I managed everything shrewdly."

"How much was paid in at the door?" asked Philip, who naturally felt interested in this phase of success.

"One hundred and forty-five dollars and a half!" answered the professor.

Philip's eyes sparkled.

"And how much will that be over and above expenses?" he asked.

"My dear Mr. de Gray, we will settle all bills, and make a fair and equitable division, in the morning. I think there will be a little more than fifty dollars to come to each of us."

"Fifty dollars for one evening's work!" repeated Philip, his eyes sparkling.

"Oh, I have done much better than that," said the professor. "I remember once at St. Louis I made for myself alone one hundred and eighty dollars net, and in Chicago a little more."

"I didn't think it was such a money-making business," said Philip, elated.

"Yes, Mr. de Gray, the American people are willing to recognize talent, when it is genuine. You are on the threshold of a great career, my dear young friend."

"And only a week since I was in the Norton Poorhouse," thought Philip. "It is certainly a case of romance in real life."

The two went to bed soon, being fatigued by their exertions. The apartment was large, and contained two beds, a larger and smaller one. The latter was occupied by our hero.

When he awoke in the morning, the sun was shining brightly into the room. Philip looked toward the opposite bed. It was empty.

"Professor Riccabocca must have got up early," he thought. "Probably he did not wish to wake me."

He dressed and went downstairs.

"Where is the professor?" he asked of the clerk.

"He started away two hours since - said he was going to take a walk. Went away without his breakfast, too. He must be fond of walking."

Philip turned pale. He was disturbed by a terrible suspicion. Had the professor gone off for good, carrying all the money with him?

CHAPTER XXIX.

BESET BY CREDITORS.

Philip was still a boy, and though he had discovered that the professor was something of a humbug, and a good deal of a braggart, it had not for a moment occurred to him that he would prove dishonest. Even now he did not want to believe it, though he was nervously apprehensive that it might prove true.

"I will take my breakfast," he said, as coolly as was possible, "and the professor will probably join me before I am through."

The clerk and the landlord thought otherwise. They were pretty well convinced that Riccabocca was dishonest, and quietly sent for those to whom the "combination" was indebted: namely, the printer and publisher of the Daily Bulletin, the agent of the music-hall, and the bill-sticker who had posted notices of the entertainment. These parties arrived while Philip was at breakfast.

"Gentlemen," said the landlord, "the boy is at breakfast. I think he is all right, but I don't know. The professor, I fear, is a swindle."

"The boy is liable for our debts," said the agent. "He

belongs to the combination."

"I am afraid he is a victim as well as you," said the landlord. "He seemed surprised to hear that the professor had gone out."

"It may all be put on. Perhaps he is in the plot, and is to meet the old fraud at some place fixed upon, and divide the booty," suggested the agent.

"The boy looks honest," said the landlord. "I like his appearance. We will see what he has to say."

So when Philip had finished his breakfast he was summoned to the parlor, where he met the creditors of the combination.

"These gentlemen," said the landlord, "have bills against you and the professor. It makes no difference whether they receive pay from you or him."

Poor Philip's heart sank within him.

"I was hoping Professor Riccabocca had settled your bills," he said. "Please show them to me."

This was done with alacrity.

Philip found that they owed five dollars for the hall, five dollars for advertising and printing, and one dollar for bill-posting - eleven dollars in all.

"Mr. Gates," said our hero uneasily, to the landlord, "did Professor Riccabocca say anything about coming back when he went out this morning?"

"He told my clerk he would be back to breakfast," said the landlord; adding, with a shrug of the shoulders: "That was two hours and a half ago. He can't be very hungry."

"He didn't pay his bill, I suppose?"

"No, of course not. He had not given up his room."

Philip became more and more uneasy.

"Didn't you know anything about his going out?" asked the landlord.

"No, sir. I was fast asleep."

"Is the professor in the habit of taking long morning walks?"

"I don't know."

"That is strange, since you travel together," remarked the publisher.

"I never saw him till day before yesterday," said Philip.

The creditors looked at each other significantly. They began to suspect that Philip also was a victim.

"Do you know how much money was received for tickets last evening?"

"About a hundred and fifty dollars."

"How much of this were you to receive?"

"Half of what was left after the bills were paid."

"Have you received it?" asked the agent.

"Not a cent," answered Philip.

"What do you think about the situation?"

"I think that Professor Riccabocca has swindled us all," answered Philip promptly.

"Our bills ought to be paid," said the agent, who was rather a hard man in his dealings.

"I agree with you," said Philip. "I wish I were able to pay them, but I have only six dollars in my possession."

"That will pay me, and leave a dollar over," suggested the agent.

"If it comes to that," said the printer, "I claim that I ought to be paid first."

"I am a poor man," said the bill-sticker. "I need my money."

Poor Philip was very much disconcerted. It was a new thing for him to owe money which he could not repay.

"Gentlemen," he said, "I have myself been cheated out of fifty dollars, at least - my share of the profits. I wish I could pay you all. I cannot do so now. Whenever I can I will certainly do it."

"You can pay us a part with the money you have," said

the agent.

"I owe Mr. Gates for nearly two days' board," he said. "That is my own affair, and I must pay him first."

"I don't see why he should be preferred to me," grumbled the agent; then, with a sudden, happy thought, as he termed it, he said: "I will tell you how you can pay us all."

"How?" asked Philip.

"You have a violin. You can sell that for enough to pay our bills."

Poor Philip! His violin was his dependence. Besides the natural attachment he felt for it, he relied upon it to secure him a living, and the thought of parting with it was bitter.

"Gentlemen," he said, "if you take my violin, I have no way of making a living. If you will consider that I, too, am a victim of this man, I think you will not wish to inflict such an injury upon me."

"I do not, for one," said the publisher. "I am not a rich man, and I need all the money that is due me, but I wouldn't deprive the boy of his violin."

"Nor I," said the bill-sticker.

"That's all very fine," said the agent; "but I am not so soft as you two. Who knows but the boy is in league with the professor?"

"I know it!" said the landlord stoutly. "The boy is all

right, or I am no judge of human nature."

"Thank you, Mr. Gates," said Philip, extending his hand to his generous defender.

"Do you expect we will let you off without paying anything?" demanded the agent harshly.

"If I live, sir, you shall lose nothing by me," said Philip.

"That won't do!" said the man coarsely. "I insist upon the fiddle being sold. I'll give five dollars for it, and call it square."

"Mr. Gunn," said the landlord, in a tone of disgust, "since you are disposed to persecute this boy, I will myself pay your bill, and trust to him to repay me when he can."

"But, Mr. Gates -" said Philip.

"I accept!" said the agent, with alacrity.

"Receipt your bill," said the landlord.

Mr. Gunn did so, and received a five-dollar bill in return.

"Now sir," said the landlord coldly, "if you have no further business here, we can dispense with your company."

"It strikes me you are rather hard on a man because he wants to be paid his honest dues!" whined Gunn, rather uncomfortably.

"We understand you, sir," said the landlord. "We have not forgotten how you turned a poor family into the street, in the dead of winter, because they could not pay their rent."

"Could I afford to give them house-room?" inquired Gunn.

"Perhaps not. At any rate, I don't feel inclined to give you house-room any longer."

Mr. Gunn slunk out of the room, under the impression that his company was no longer desired.

"Mr. Gray," said the publisher, "I hope you don't class me with the man who has just gone out. I would sooner never be paid than deprive you of your violin. Let the account stand, and if you are ever able to pay me half of my bill - your share - I shall be glad to receive it."

"Thank you, sir!" said Philip, "You shall not repent your confidence in me."

"I say ditto to my friend, the publisher," said the bill-poster.

"Wait a moment, gentlemen," said Philip. "There is a bare possibility that I can do something for you."

For the first time since he left Norton he thought of the letter which he was not to open till he was fifty miles from Norton.

"Mr. Gates," he said, "can you tell me how far Norton is from here?"

"About sixty miles," answered the landlord in surprise.

"Then it's all right."

CHAPTER XXX.

A TIMELY GIFT.

The reader has not forgotten that Farmer Lovett, when Philip refused to accept any compensation for assisting to frustrate the attempt at burglary, handed him a sealed envelope, which he requested him not to open till he was fifty miles away from Norton.

Philip had carried this about in his pocket ever since. He had thought of it as likely to contain some good advice at the time; but it had since occurred to him that the farmer had not had time to write down anything in that line.

He was disposed to think that the mysterious envelope might contain a five-dollar bill, as a slight acknowledgment of his services.

Though Philip had declined receiving any payment, it did seem to him now that this amount of money would relieve him from considerable embarrassment. He therefore drew a penknife from his pocket and cut open the envelope.

What was his amazement when he drew out three bills - two twenties and a ten - fifty dollars in all! There was a slip of paper, on which was written, in pencil:

"Don't hesitate to use this money, if you need it, as you doubtless will. I can spare it as well as not, and shall be glad if it proves of use to one who has done me a great service. JOHN LOVETT."

"What's that!" asked the landlord, regarding Philip with interest.

"Some money which I did not know I possessed," answered Philip.

"How much is there?"

"Fifty dollars."

"And you didn't know you had it?" asked the publisher - rather incredulously, it must be owned.

"No, sir; I was told not to open this envelope till I was fifty miles away from where it was given me. Of course, Mr. Gates, I am now able to pay all my bills, and to repay you for what you handed Mr. Gunn."

"I am pleased with your good fortune," said the landlord cordially.

"Thank you, sir."

"But I am sorry your knavish partner has cheated you out of so much money."

"I shall make him pay it if I can," said Philip resolutely.

"I approve your pluck, and I wish you success."

"He owes you money, too, Mr. Gates. Give me the bill, and I will do my best to collect it."

"If you collect it, you may have it," said Gates. "I don't care much for the money, but I should like to have the scamp compelled to fork it over."

"I wish I knew where he was likely to be," said Philip.

"He may go to Knoxville," suggested the publisher.

"How far is that?"

"Ten miles."

"What makes you think he will go to Knoxville?" asked the landlord.

"He may think of giving a performance there. It is a pretty large place."

"But wouldn't he be afraid to do it, after the pranks he has played here?"

"Perhaps so. At any rate, he is very likely to go there."

"I will go there and risk it," said Philip. "He needn't think he is going to get off so easily, even if it is only a boy he has cheated."

"That's the talk, Mr. Gray!" said the landlord. "How are you going?" he asked, a minute later.

"I can walk ten miles well enough," answered Philip.

He had considerable money now, but he reflected that

he should probably need it all, especially if he did not succeed in making the professor refund, and decided that it would be well to continue to practice economy.

"I have no doubt you can," said the landlord, but it will be better not to let the professor get too much the start of you. I will myself have a horse harnessed, and take you most of the distance in my buggy."

"But, Mr. Gates, won't it be putting you to a great deal of trouble?"

"Not at all. I shall enjoy a ride this morning, and the road to Knoxville is a very pleasant one."

"Let me pay something for the ride, then."

"Not a cent. You will need all your money, and I can carry you just as well as not," said the landlord heartily.

"I am very fortunate in such a kind friend," said Philip gratefully.

"Oh, it isn't worth talking about! Here, Jim, go out and harness the horse directly."

When the horse was brought round, Philip was all ready, and jumped in.

"Would you like to drive, Mr. Gray?" asked the landlord.

"Yes," answered Philip, with alacrity.

"Take the lines, then," said the landlord.

Most boys of Philip's age are fond of driving, and our hero was no exception to the rule, as the landlord supposed.

"You'll promise not to upset me," said Mr. Gates, smiling. "I am getting stout, and the consequences might be serious."

"Oh, I am used to driving," said Philip, "and I will take care not to tip over."

The horse was a good one, and to Philip's satisfaction, went over the road in good style.

Philip enjoyed driving, but, of course, his mind could not help dwelling on the special object of his journey.

"I hope we are on the right track," he said. "I shouldn't like to miss the professor."

"You will soon know, at any rate," said Gates. "It seems to me," he continued, "that Riccabocca made a great mistake in running off with that money."

"He thought it would be safe to cheat a boy."

"Yes; but admitting all that, you two were likely to make money. In Wilkesville your profits were a hundred dollars in one evening. Half of that belonged to the professor, at any rate. He has lost his partner, and gained only fifty dollars, which would not begin to pay him for your loss."

"Perhaps he thought he would draw as well alone."

"Then he is very much mistaken. To tell the plain truth,

our people thought very little of his share of the performance. I saw some of them laughing when he was ranting away. It was you they enjoyed hearing."

"I am glad of that," said Philip, gratified.

"There's no humbug about your playing. You understand it. It was you that saved the credit of the evening, and sent people away well satisfied."

"I am glad of that, at any rate, even if I didn't get a cent for my playing," said Philip, well pleased.

"The money's the practical part of it," said the landlord. "Of course, I am glad when travelers like my hotel, but if they should run off without paying, like the professor, I shouldn't enjoy it so much."

"No, I suppose not," said Philip, with a laugh.

They had ridden some seven miles, and were, therefore, only three miles from Knoxville, without the slightest intimation as to whether or not they were on the right track.

To be sure, they had not expected to obtain any clue so soon, but it would have been very satisfactory, of course, to obtain one.

A little farther on they saw approaching a buggy similar to their own, driven by a man of middle age. It turned out to be an acquaintance of the landlord's, and the two stopped to speak.

"Going to Knoxville on business, Mr. Gates?" asked the newcomer.

"Well, not exactly. I am driving this young man over. By the way, have you seen anything of a tall man, with long, black hair, dressed in black?"

"Yes. Do you want to see him?"

"This young man has some business with him. Where did you see him?"

"He arrived at our hotel about an hour since, I calculate."

Philip's heart bounded with satisfaction at this important news.

"Did he put up there?"

"Yes. I believe he is going to give a reading this evening."

"Thank you!"

"The professor must be a fool!" said the landlord, as they drove away.

"I begin to think so myself," replied Philip.

"That's all in our favor, however. We shall get back that money yet."

The horse was put to his speed, and in fifteen minutes they reached Knoxville.

CHAPTER XXXI.

THE PROFESSOR'S FLIGHT.

Professor Lorenzo Riccabocca was not a wise man. It would have been much more to his interest to deal honestly with Philip, paying his share of the profits of the first performance, and retaining his services as associate and partner.

But the professor was dazzled by the money, and unwilling to give it up. Moreover, he had the vanity to think that he would draw nearly as well alone, thus retaining in his own hands the entire proceeds of any entertainments he might give.

When he met Philip on the road he was well-nigh penniless. Now, including the sum of which he had defrauded our hero and his creditors in Wilkesville, he had one hundred and fifty dollars.

When the professor went to bed, he had not formed the plan of deserting Philip; but, on awaking in the morning, it flashed upon him as an excellent step which would put money in his pocket.

He accordingly rose, dressed himself quietly, and, with one cautious look at Philip - who was fast asleep - descended the stairs to the office.

Only the bookkeeper was in the office.

"You are stirring early, professor," he said.

"Yes," answered Riccabocca, "I generally take a morning walk, to get an appetite for breakfast."

"My appetite comes without the walk," said the bookkeeper, smiling.

"If Mr. de Gray comes downstairs, please tell him I will be back soon," said Riccabocca.

The bookkeeper readily promised to do this, not having the slightest suspicion that the distinguished professor was about to take French leave.

When Professor Riccabocca had walked half a mile he began to feel faint. His appetite had come.

"I wish I had stopped to breakfast," he reflected. "I don't believe De Gray will be down for an hour or two."

It was too late to go back and repair his mistake. That would spoil all. He saw across the street a baker's shop, just opening for the day, and this gave him an idea.

He entered, bought some rolls, and obtained a glass of milk, and, fortified with these, he resumed his journey.

He had walked three miles, when he was over-taken by a farm wagon, which was going his way.

He hailed the driver - a young man of nineteen or thereabouts - ascertained that he was driving to

Knoxville, and, for a small sum, secured passage there.

This brings us to the point of time when Philip and Mr. Gates drove up to the hotel at Knoxville.

"I can see the professor," said Philip, in eager excitement, when they had come within a few rods of the inn.

"Where is he?"

"He is in the office, sitting with his back to the front window. I wonder what he will have to say for himself?"

"So do I," said the landlord curiously.

"Shall we go in together?" questioned Philip.

"No; let us surprise him a little. I will drive around to the sheds back of the hotel, and fasten my horse. Then we will go round to the front, and you can go in, while I stand outside, ready to appear a little later."

Philip thought this a good plan. He enjoyed the prospect of confronting the rogue who had taken advantage of his inexperience, and attempted such a bold scheme of fraud. He didn't feel in the least nervous, or afraid to encounter the professor, though Riccabocca was a man and he but a boy. When all was ready, Philip entered through the front door, which was open, and, turning into the office, stood before the astonished professor.

The latter started in dismay at the sight of our hero. He thought he might be quietly eating breakfast ten miles away, unsuspiciously waiting for his return. Was his brilliant scheme to fail? He quickly took his resolution - a foolish one. He would pretend not to know Philip.

"Well, Professor Riccabocca," Philip said, in a sarcastic tone, "you took rather a long walk this morning."

The professor looked at him vacantly.

"Were you addressing me?" he inquired.

"Yes, sir," answered Philip, justly provoked.

"I haven't the pleasure of your acquaintance, young man."

"I wish I hadn't the pleasure of yours," retorted Philip.

"Do you come here to insult me?" demanded Riccabocca, frowning.

"I came here to demand my share of the money received for the entertainment last evening, as well as the money paid for the hall, the printer, and bill-poster."

"You must be crazy!" said Riccabocca, shrugging his shoulders. "I don't know you. I don't owe you any money."

"Do you mean to say we didn't give an entertainment together last evening at Wilkesville?" asked Philip, rather taken aback by the man's sublime impudence.

"My young friend, you have been dreaming. Prove

what you say and I will admit your claim."

Up to this point those present, deceived by the professor's coolness, really supposed him to be in the right. That was what Riccabocca anticipated, and hoped to get off before the discovery of the truth could be made. But he did not know that Philip had a competent witness at hand.

"Mr. Gates!" called Philip.

The portly landlord of the Wilkesville Hotel entered the room, and Riccaboeca saw that the game was up.

"Mr. Gates, will you be kind enough to convince this gentleman that he owes me money?" asked Philip.

"I think he won't deny it now," said Gates significantly. "He walked off from my hotel this morning, leaving his bill unpaid. Professor Riccabocca, it strikes me you had better settle with us, unless you wish to pass the night in the lockup."

Professor Riccabocca gave a forced laugh.

"Why, Mr. de Gray," he said, "you ought to have known that I was only playing a trick on you."

"I supposed you were," said Philip.

"No, I don't mean that. I was only pretending I didn't know you, to see if I could act naturally enough, to deceive you."

"Why did you desert me?" asked Philip suspiciously.

"I started to take a walk - didn't the bookkeeper tell you? - and finding a chance to ride over here, thought I would do so, and make arrangements for our appearance here. Of course, I intended to come back, and pay our good friend, the landlord, and give you your share of the common fund."

Neither Gates nor Philip believed a word of this. It seemed to them quite too transparent.

"You may as well pay us now, Professor Riccabocca," said the landlord dryly.

"I hope you don't suspect my honor or integrity," said Riccabocca, appearing to be wounded at the thought.

"Never mind about that," said Mr. Gates shortly. "Actions speak louder than words."

"I am quite ready to settle - quite," said the professor. "The money is in my room. I will go up and get it."

There seemed to be no objection to this, and our two friends saw him ascend the staircase to the second story. Philip felt pleased to think that he had succeeded in his quest, for his share of the concert money would be nearly seventy dollars. That, with the balance of the money; received from Farmer Lovett, would make over a hundred dollars.

They waited five minutes, and the professor did not come down.

"What can keep him?" said Philip.

Just then one of the hostlers entered and caught what

our hero had said.

"A man has just run out of the back door," he said, "and is cutting across the fields at a great rate."

"He must have gone down the back stairs," said the clerk.

"In what direction would he go?" asked Philip hastily.

"To the railroad station. There is a train leaves in fifteen minutes."

"What shall we do, Mr. Gates?" asked Philip, in dismay.

"Jump into my buggy. We'll get to the depot before the train starts. We must intercept the rascal."

CHAPTER XXXII.

THE RACE ACROSS FIELDS.

It so happened that Professor Riccabocca had once before visited Knoxville, and remembered the location of the railroad station. Moreover, at the hotel, before the arrival of Philip, he had consulted a schedule of trains posted up in the office, and knew that one would leave precisely at ten o'clock.

The impulse to leave town by this train was sudden. He had in his pocket the wallet containing the hundred and fifty dollars, of which a large part belonged to Philip, and could have settled at once, without the trouble of going upstairs to his room.

He only asked leave to go up there in order to gain time for thought. At the head of the staircase he saw another narrower flight of stairs descending to the back of the house. That gave him the idea of eluding his two creditors by flight.

I have said before that Professor Riccabocca was not a wise man, or he would have reflected that he was only postponing the inevitable reckoning. Moreover, it would destroy the last chance of making an arrangement with Philip to continue the combination, which thus far had proved so profitable.

The professor did not take this into consideration, but dashed down the back stairs, and opened the back door into the yard.

"Do you want anything, sir?" asked a maidservant, eyeing the professor suspiciously.

"Nothing at all, my good girl," returned the professor.

"You seem to be in a hurry," she continued, with renewed suspicion.

"So I am. I am in a great hurry to meet an engagement."

"Why didn't you go out the front door?" asked the girl.

"Oh, bother! What business is it of yours?" demanded the professor impatiently.

And, not stopping for further inquiries, he vaulted over a fence and took his way across the fields to the station.

"Here, Sam," called the girl, her suspicions confirmed that something was wrong, "go after that man as fast as you can!"

This was addressed to a boy who was employed at the hotel to go on errands and do odd jobs.

"What's he done?" asked Sam.

"I don't know; but he's either run off without paying his bill, or he's stolen something."

"What good'll it do me to chase him?" asked Sam.

"If he's cheated master, he'll pay you for catching the man."

"That's so," thought Sam. "Besides, I'll be a detective, just like that boy I read about in the paper. I'm off!"

Fired by youthful ambition, Sam also vaulted the fence, and ran along the foot-path in pursuit of the professor.

Lorenzo Riccabocca did not know he was pursued. He felt himself so safe from this, on account of the secrecy of his departure, that he never took the trouble to look behind him. He knew the way well enough, for the fields he was crossing were level, and half a mile away, perhaps a little more, he could see the roof of the brown-painted depot, which was his destination. Once there, he would buy a ticket, get on the train, and get started away from Knoxville before the troublesome acquaintances who were waiting for him to come down-stairs had any idea where he was gone.

The professor ran at a steady, even pace, looking straight before him. His eyes were fixed on the haven of his hopes, and he did not notice a stone, of considerable size, which lay in his path. The result was that he stumbled over it, and fell forward with considerable force. He rose, jarred and sore, but there was no time to take account of his physical damages. He must wait till he got on the train.

The force with which he was thrown forward was such that the wallet was thrown from his pocket, and fell in the grass beside the path. The professor went on his way, quite unconscious of his loss, but there were other eyes that did not overlook it.

Sam, who was thirty rods behind, noticed Professor Riccabocca's fall, and he likewise noticed the wallet when he reached the spot of the catastrophe.

"My eyes!" he exclaimed, opening those organs wide in delight; "here's luck! The old gentleman has dropped his pocketbook. Most likely it's stolen. I'll carry it back and give it to Mr. Perry."

Sam very sensibly decided that it wasn't worth while to continue the pursuit, now that the thief, as he supposed Riccabocca to be, had dropped his booty.

Sam was led by curiosity to open the wallet. When he saw the thick roll of bills, he was filled with amazement and delight.

"Oh, what a rascal he was!" ejaculated the boy. "I guess he's been robbing a safe. I wonder how much is here?"

He was tempted to sit down on the grass and count the bills, but he was prevented by the thought that the professor might discover his loss, and returning upon his track, question him as to whether he had found it. Sam determined that he wouldn't give it up, at any rate.

"I guess I could wrastle with him," he thought. "He looks rather spindlin', but then he's bigger than I am, and he might lick me, after all."

I desire to say emphatically that Sam was strictly honest, and never for a moment thought of appropriating any of the money to his own use. He felt that as a detective he had been successful, and this made him feel proud and happy.

"I may as well go home," he said. "If he's stolen this money from Mr. Perry, I'll come in for a reward."

Sam did not hurry, however. He was not now in pursuit of any one, and could afford to loiter and recover his breath.

Meanwhile, Professor Riccabocca, in happy unconsciousness of his loss, continued his run to the station. He arrived there breathless, and hurried to the ticket-office.

"Give me a ticket to Chambersburg," he said.

"All right, sir. Ninety cents."

If Riccabocca had been compelled to take out his wallet, he would at once have discovered his loss, and the ticket would not have been bought. But he had a two-dollar bill in his vest, and it was out of this that he paid for the ticket to Chambersburg. Armed with the ticket, he waited anxiously for the train. He had five minutes to wait - five anxious moments in which his flight might be discovered. He paced the platform, looking out anxiously for the train.

At length he heard the welcome sound of the approaching locomotive. The train came to a stop, and among the first to enter it was the eminent elocutionist. He took a seat beside the window looking out toward the village. What did he see that brought such an anxious look in his face?

A buggy was approaching the depot at breakneck speed. It contained Mr. Gates, the landlord, and the young musician. Mr. Gates was lashing the horse, and evidently was exceedingly anxious to arrive at the depot before the train started.

Beads of perspiration stood on the anxious brow of the professor. His heart was filled with panic terror.

"The girl must have told them of my flight," he said to himself. "Oh, why didn't I think to give her a quarter to keep her lips closed? Why doesn't the train start?"

The buggy was only about ten rods away. It looked as if Philip and his companion would be able to intercept the fugitive.

Just then the scream of the locomotive was heard. The train began to move. Professor Riccabocca gave a sigh of relief.

"I shall escape them after all," he said triumphantly, to himself.

He opened the window, and, with laughing face, nodded to his pursuers.

"We've lost him!" said Philip, in a tone of disappointment. "What can we do?"

"Find out where he is going, and telegraph to have him stopped," said Mr. Gates. "That will put a spoke in his wheel."

CHAPTER XXXIII.

THE LOST WALLET.

Mr. Gates was acquainted with the depot-master, and lost no time in seeking him.

"Too late for the train?" asked the latter, who observed in the landlord evidences of haste.

"Not for the train, but for one of the passengers by the train," responded the landlord. "Did you take notice of a man dressed in a shabby suit of black, wearing a soft hat and having very long black hair?"

"Yes."

"Where is he going?" asked Mr. Gates eagerly.

"He bought a ticket for Chambersburg."

"Ha! Well, I want you to telegraph for me to Chambersburg."

The station-master was also the telegraph-operator, as it chanced.

"Certainly. Just write out your message and I will send it at once."

Mr. Gates telegraphed to a deputy sheriff at Chambersburg to be at the depot on arrival of the train, and to arrest and detain the professor till he could communicate further with him.

"Now," said he, turning to Philip, "I think we shall he able to stop the flight of your friend."

"Don't call him my friend," said Philip. "He is anything but a friend."

"You are right there. Well, I will amend and call him your partner. Now, Mr. de Gray -"

"My name is Gray - not de Gray. The professor put in the 'de' because he thought it would sound foreign."

"I presume you have as much right to the name as he has to the title of professor," said Gates.

"I don't doubt it," returned Philip, smiling.

"Well, as I was about to say, we may as well go back to the hotel, and await the course of events. I think there is some chance of your getting your money back."

When they reached the hotel, they found a surprise in store for them.

Sam had carried the professor's wallet to Mr. Perry, and been told by them to wait and hand it in person to Philip and his friend, Mr. Gates, who were then at the depot.

When they arrived, Sam was waiting on the stoop,

wallet in hand.

"What have you got there, Sam?" asked Mr. Gates, who often came to Knoxville, and knew the boy. "It's the wallet of that man you were after," said Sam.

"How did you get it?" asked Philip eagerly.

"I chased him 'cross lots," said Sam.

"You didn't knock him over and take the wallet from him, did you, Sam?" asked Mr. Gates.

"Not so bad as that," answered Sam, grinning. "You see, he tripped over a big rock, and came down on his hands and knees. The wallet jumped out of his pocket, but he didn't see it. I picked it up and brought it home."

"Didn't he know you were chasing him?"

"I guess not. He never looked back."

"What made you think of running after him?"

"One of the girls told me to. The way he ran out of the back door made her think there was something wrong."

"Suppose he had turned round?"

"I guess I could have wrastled with him," said Sam, to the amusement of those who heard him.

"It is well you were not obliged to."

"Who shall I give the wallet to?" asked Sam.

"Mr. Gray, here, is the professor's partner, and half the money belongs to him. You can give it to him."

"Have I a right to take it?" asked Philip, who did not wish to do anything unlawful.

He was assured that, as the business partner of the professor, he had as much right as Riccabocca to the custody of the common fund.

"But half of it belongs to the professor."

"He'll come back for it, in the custody of the sheriff. I didn't think I was doing the man a good turn when I telegraphed to have him stopped."

The first thing Philip did was to take from his own funds a five-dollar bill, which he tendered to Sam.

"Is it all for me?" asked the boy, his eyes sparkling his joy.

"Yes; but for you I should probably have lost a good deal more. Thank you, besides."

And Philip offered his hand to Sam, who grasped it fervently.

"I say, you're a tip-top chap," said Sam. "You ain't like a man that lost a pocketbook last summer, with a hundred dollars in it, and gave me five cents for finding it."

"No; I hope I'm not as mean as that," said Philip, smiling.

He opened the wallet and found a memorandum containing an exact statement of the proceeds of the concert. This was of great service to him, as it enabled him to calculate his own share of the profits.

The aggregate receipts were one hundred and fifty dollars and fifty cents. Deducting bills paid, viz.:

Rent of hall $5.00

Printing, etc........... 5.00

Bill-poster 1.00

Total $11.00

there was a balance of $138.50, of which Philip was entitled to one-half, namely, $69.25. This he took, together with the eleven dollars which he had himself paid to the creditors of the combination, and handed the wallet, with the remainder of the money, to Mr. Perry, landlord of the Knoxville Hotel, with a request that he would keep it till called for by Professor Riccabocca.

"You may hand me three dollars and a half, Mr. Perry," said Mr. Gates. "That is the amount the professor owes me for a day and three-quarters at my hotel. If he makes a fuss, you can tell him he is quite at liberty to go to law about it."

Meanwhile, where was the professor, and when did he discover his loss?

After the train was a mile or two on its way he felt in his pocket for the wallet, meaning to regale himself with a sight of its contents - now, as he considered, all his own.

Thrusting his hand into his pocket, it met - vacancy.

Pale with excitement, he continued his search, extending it to all his other pockets. But the treasure had disappeared!

Professor Riccabocca was panic-stricken. He could hardly suppress a groan.

A good woman sitting opposite, judging from his pallor that he was ill, leaned over and asked, in a tone of sympathy:

"Are you took sick?"

"No, ma'am," answered the professor sharply.

"You look as if you was goin' to have a fit," continued the sympathizing woman. "Jest take some chamomile tea the first chance you get. It's the sovereignest thing I know of -"

"Will chamomile tea bring back a lost pocket-book?" demanded the professor sharply.

"Oh, Lor'! you don't say you lost your money?"

"Yes, I do!" said Riccabocca, glaring at her.

"Oh, dear! do you think there's pickpockets in the car?" asked the old lady nervously.

"Very likely," answered the professor tragically.

The good woman kept her hand in her pocket all the rest of the way, eyeing all her fellow passengers sharply.

But the professor guessed the truth. He had lost his wallet when he stumbled in the field. He was in a fever of impatience to return and hunt for it. Instead of going on to Chambersburg, he got out at the next station - five miles from Knoxville - and walked back on the railroad-track. So it happened that the telegram did no good.

The professor walked back to the hotel across the fields, hunting diligently, but saw nothing of the lost wallet. He entered the hotel, footsore, weary, and despondent. The first person he saw was Philip, sitting tranquilly in the office.

"Did you just come down from your room?" asked our hero coolly.

"I am a most unfortunate man!" sighed Riccabocca, sinking into a seat.

"What's the matter?"

"I've lost all our money."

"I am glad you say 'our money.' I began to think you considered it all yours. Didn't I see you on the train?"

"I had a bad headache," stammered the professor, "and I didn't know what I was doing."

"Does riding in the cars benefit your head?"

Professor Riccabocca looked confused.

"The wallet was found," said Philip, not wishing to keep him any longer in suspense.

"Where is it?" asked the professor eagerly.

"Mr. Perry will give it to you. I have taken out my share of the money, and Mr. Gates has received the amount of his bill. It would have been better for you to attend to these matters yourselff like an honest man."

Professor Riccabocca was so overjoyed to have back his own money that he made no fuss about Philip's proceedings. Indeed, his own intended dishonesty was so apparent that it would have required even more assurance than he possessed to make a protest.

CHAPTER XXXIV.

A NEW BUSINESS PROPOSAL.

Professor Riccabocca put the wallet in his pocket with a sigh of satisfaction. There were still sixty dollars or more in it, and it was long since he had been so rich.

He began to think now that it might be well to revive the combination. There was some doubt, however, as to how Philip would receive the proposal.

He looked at his young partner and was not much encouraged. He felt that he must conciliate him.

"Mr. de Gray," he began.

"Call me Gray. My name is not de Gray."

"Well, Mr. Gray, then. I hope you don't have any hard feelings."

"About what?" inquired Philip, surveying the professor curiously.

"About - the past," stammered the professor.

"You mean about your running off with my money?" returned Philip plainly.

Professor Riccabocca winced. He did not quite like this form of statement. "I am afraid you misjudge me," he said, rather confused.

"I shall be glad to listen to any explanation you have to offer," said our hero.

"I will explain it all to you, in time," said the professor, recovering his old assurance. "In the meantime, I have a proposition to make to you."

"What is it?"

"Suppose we give an entertainment in Knoxville - on the same terms as the last."

"I shouldn't think you would like to appear before an audience here, Professor Riccabocca."

"Why not?"

"Before night everybody will have heard of your running away with the proceeds of the last concert."

"Public men are always misjudged. They must expect it," said the professor, with the air of a martyr.

"I should think you would be more afraid of being justly judged."

"Mr. Gray," said the professor, "I have done wrong, I admit; but it was under the influence of neuralgia. When I have a neuralgic headache, I am not myself. I do things which, in a normal condition, I should not dream of. I am the victim of a terrible physical malady."

Philip did not believe a word of this, but he felt amused at the professor's singular excuse.

"Come, Mr. Gray, what do you say?"

"I think I must decline," returned Philip.

But here Professor Riccabocca received unexpected help.

Mr. Perry, the landlord, who had listened to the colloquy, approached the two speakers and said:

"Gentlemen, I have a proposal to make to you both."

Both Philip and the professor looked up, with interest.

"Some of the young men in the village," said the landlord, "have formed a literary club, meeting weekly. They have hired and furnished a room over one of our stores, provided it with, games and subscribed for a few periodicals. They find, however, that the outlay has been greater than they anticipated and are in debt. I have been talking with the secretary, and he thinks he would like to engage you to give an entertainment, the proceeds, beyond a fixed sum, to go to the benefit of the club. What do you say?"

"When is it proposed to have the entertainment?" asked Philip.

"I suppose we should have to name to-morrow evening, in order to advertise it sufficiently."

"I am willing to make any engagement that will suit the club," said Philip.

"And I, too," said Professor Riccabocca.

"The secretary authorizes me to offer you ten dollars each, and to pay your hotel expenses in the meantime," said Mr. Perry.

"That is satisfactory," said our hero.

"I agree," said the professor.

"Then I will at once notify the secretary, and he will take steps to advertise the entertainment."

Ten dollars was a small sum compared with what Philip had obtained for his evening in Wilkesville, but a week since he would have regarded it as very large for one week's work. He felt that it was for his interest to accept the proposal.

He secretly resolved that if the entertainment should not prove as successful as was anticipated, he would give up a part of the sum which was promised him for his services.

Professor Riccabocca assented the more readily to the proposal, because he thought it might enable him again to form a business alliance with our hero, from whom his conduct had estranged him.

"Suppose we take a room together, Mr. de Gray," he said, with an ingratiating smile.

"Gray, if you please, professor. I don't like sailing under false colors."

"Excuse me; the force of habit, you know. Well, do

you agree?"

"The professor has more assurance than any man I ever heard of," thought Philip. "You must excuse me, professor," he said. "After what has happened, I should feel safer in a room by myself."

"Why will you dwell upon the past, Mr. Gray?" said the professor reproachfully.

"Because I am prudent, and learn from experience," answered Philip.

"I assure you, you will have nothing to complain of," said Riccabocca earnestly. "If we are together, we can consult about the program."

"We shall have plenty of time to do that during the day, professor."

"Then you don't care to room with me?" said Riccabocca, looking disappointed.

"No, I don't."

"What are you afraid of?"

"I am afraid you might have an attack of neuralgic headache during the night," said Philip, laughing.

Professor Riccabocca saw that it would be of no use for him to press the request, and allowed himself to be conducted to the same room which he had so unceremoniously left a short time before.

During the afternoon, Philip had a call from John

Turner, the secretary of the Young Men's Club. He was a pleasant, straightforward young man, of perhaps twenty.

"We are very much obliged to you, Mr. Gray," he said, "for kindly consenting to play for our benefit."

"It is for my interest," said Philip frankly. "I may as well remain here and earn ten dollars as to be idle."

"But you made a great deal more, I understand, in Wilkesville?"

"Yes; but I might not be as fortunate here. I had not intended to appear here at all, and should not have done so unless you had invited me. How many have you in your club?"

"Only about twenty-five, so far, and some of us are not able to pay much."

"How long has your club been formed?" asked Philip.

"Only about three months. We wanted a place where we could meet together socially in the evening, and have a good time. Before, we had only the stores and barrooms to go to, and there we were tempted to drink. Our club was started in the interests of temperance, and we can see already that it is exerting a good influence."

"Then I am very glad to assist you," said Philip cordially.

"You must come round and see our room. Are you at leisure now?"

"Yes, Mr. Turner."

Philip accompanied his new friend to the neatly furnished room leased by the society. He was so well pleased with its appearance that he thought he should himself like to belong to such an association, whenever he found a permanent home. At present he was only a wanderer.

"Our debt is thirty-four dollars," said the secretary. "You may not think it large, but it's large for us."

"I hope our entertainment will enable you to clear it off."

"If it should it will give us new courage."

On the evening of the next day Philip and the professor entered the hall engaged for the entertainment, and took seats on the platform.

The hall was well filled, the scale of prices being the same as at Wilkesville.

"Mr. Gray," whispered the secretary joyfully, "it is a great success! After paying all bills the club will clear fifty dollars."

"I am delighted to hear it," said Philip.

The professor commenced the entertainment, and was followed by Philip.

As Philip began to play his attention was drawn to three persons who were entering the hall.

These were a lady, a little girl, and a stout gentleman, in whom Philip, almost petrified with amazement, recognized his old acquaintance, Squire Pope, of Norton, who had shown himself so anxious to provide him a home in the poor-house.

CHAPTER XXXV.

SQUIRE POPE IS AMAZED.

Though Philip did not know it, it chanced that Squire Pope's only sister, Mrs. Cunningham, lived in Knoxville. She was a widow, fairly well off, with a young daughter, Carrie - a girl of twelve. Squire Pope had long thought of visiting his sister, and happening about this time to have a little business in a town near-by, he decided to carry out his long-deferred plan. He arrived by the afternoon train, in time for supper.

"I am glad you are here to-night, brother," said Mrs. Cunningham.

"Why particularly to-night, Sister Ellen?" asked the squire.

"Because there is to be an entertainment for the benefit of the Young Men's Literary Club. It is expected to be very interesting."

"What sort of an entertainment, Ellen?" asked the squire.

"The celebrated elocutionist, Professor Riccabocca, is to give some readings -"

"Riccabocca!" repeated the squire, in a musing tone. "I can't say I ever heard of him."

"Nor I; but I hear he's very celebrated."

"Is there anything else?"

"Yes, there's a young musician going to play. He is said to be wonderful. He plays on the violin."

"He's a very handsome boy," said Carrie enthusiastically. "He's staying at the hotel. I saw him this afternoon when I was passing."

"So he's good-looking, is he, Carrie?" asked the squire, laughing.

"He's ever so good-looking," answered Carrie emphatically.

"Then we must certainly go, for Carrie's sake," said the squire.

Squire Pope had not the slightest idea that the young musician, about whom his niece spoke so enthusiastically, was the boy whom he had so recently persecuted.

If Carrie had mentioned his name, the secret would have been out, but she had not yet heard it.

In honor of her brother's arrival, Mrs. Cunningham prepared a more elaborate supper than usual, and to this it was owing that the three entered the hall late, just as Philip was about to commence playing.

The squire and his companions were obliged to take seats some distance away from the platform, and as his eyesight was poor, he didn't immediately recognize as an old acquaintance the boy who was standing before the audience with his violin in his hand.

"That's he! That's the young violin-player!" whispered Carrie, in a tone of delight. "Isn't he handsome, uncle!"

"Wait till I get my glasses on," said the squire, fumbling in his pocket for his spectacle-case.

Adjusting his glasses, Squire Pope directed a glance at the stage. He instantly recognized Philip, and his surprise was boundless. He gave a sudden start.

"By gracious, I couldn't have believed it!" he ejaculated.

"Couldn't have believed what, brother?" asked Mrs. Cunningham.

"I know that boy!" he said, in a tone of excitement.

"You know him, uncle?" said Carrie, delighted. "Then you must introduce me to him. I want to meet him ever so much. Where did you ever see him?"

"Where did I see him? I'm his guardian. He ran away from me a little more than a week since, and I never knew where he went."

"You the guardian of the wonderful boy-player?" said Carrie, astonished. "Isn't it strange?"

"His father died a short time since and left him in my

care," said the squire, not scrupling to make a misstatement. "But I'll tell you more about it when the performance is over."

When Philip first saw Squire Pope entering the hall it disconcerted him, but he reflected that the squire really had no authority over him, and consequently he had nothing to fear from him.

Should his pretended guardian make any effort to recover him, he was resolved to make a desperate resistance, and even, if necessary, to invoke the help of the law.

Meanwhile, his pride stimulated him to play his best, and the hearty applause of the audience when he had finished his piece encouraged him.

As he was bowing his thanks he could not help directing a triumphant glance at Squire Pope, who was carefully scrutinizing him through his gold-bowed spectacles.

He was glad that the squire had a chance to see for himself that he was well able to make his own way, with the help of the violin of which the Norton official had attempted to deprive him.

In truth, Squire Pope, who knew little of Philip's playing, except that he did play, was amazed to find him so proficient. Instead, however, of concluding that a boy so gifted was abundantly able to "paddle his own canoe," as the saying is, he was the more resolved to carry him back to Norton, and to take into his own care any the boy might have earned. In the middle of the entertainment was a recess of ten minutes, which most of the audience spent in conversation.

Miss Carrie began again to speak of Philip.

"Oh, - uncle," she said, "I'm so glad you know that lovely boy-player! He is earning lots of money."

"Is he!" asked the squire, pricking up his ears. "Who told you so?"

"One of the young men that belongs to the club told me they were to pay him ten dollars for playing to-night."

"Ten dollars!" ejaculated the squire, in amazement. "I don't believe it! It's ridiculous!"

"Oh, yes, it is true!" said Mrs. Cunningham. "John Turner told Carrie; and he is secretary, and ought to know."

"That isn't all," continued Carrie. "Mr. Turner says it is very kind of Mr. Gray -"

"Mr. Gray!" repeated the squire, amused.

"Well, Philip, then. I suppose you call him Philip, as you are his guardian."

"Well, what were you going to say?"

"Mr. Turner says that it is very kind of Philip to play for so little, for he made a good deal more money by his entertainment in Wilkesville."

"Did he give a concert in Wilkesville?" asked the

squire quickly.

"Yes, he and the professor. He was liked very much there."

"And you heard that he made a good deal of money there?"

"Yes; lots of it."

"Then," thought the squire, "he must have considerable money with him. As his guardian I ought to have the care of it. He's a boy, and isn't fit to have the charge of money. It's very lucky I came here just as I did. It's my duty, as his guardian, to look after him."

The squire determined to seek an interview with our hero as soon as the entertainment was over.

CHAPTER XXXVI.

THE PRETENDED GUARDIAN.

Philip played with excellent effect, and his efforts were received with as much favor at Knoxville as at Wilkesville. He was twice encored, and at the end of each of his selections he was greeted with applause.

As for Professor Riccabocca, people hardly knew what to make of him. He was as eccentric and extravagant as ever, and his recitations were received with good-natured amusement. He didn't lack for applause, however. There were some boys on the front seats who applauded him, just for the fun of it. Though the applause was ironical, the professor persuaded himself that it was genuine, and posed before the audience at each outburst, with his hand on his heart, and his head bent so far over that he seemed likely to lose his balance.

"We are making a grand success, Mr. Gray," he said, during the interval of ten minutes already referred to. "Did you notice how they applauded me?"

"Yes," answered Philip, with a smile.

"They evidently appreciate true genius. It reminds me of the ovation they gave me at Cincinnati last winter."

"Does it?" asked Philip, still smiling.

"Yes. I was a great favorite in that intellectual city. By the way, I noticed that they seemed well pleased with your playing also."

This he said carelessly, as if Philip's applause was not to be compared to his.

"Yes, they treat me very kindly," answered Philip.

"You are fortunate in having me to introduce you to the public," said the professor emphatically. "The name of Riccabocca is so well known, that it is of great advantage to you."

The professor deluded himself with the idea that he was a great elocutionist, and that the public rated him as highly as he did himself. When anything occurred that did not seem to favor this view, he closed his eyes to it, preferring to believe that he was a popular favorite.

"I hope I shall never be so deceived about myself," thought Philip.

When the entertainment was over, Mr. Caswell, president of the club, came up to Philip and said cordially:

"Mr. Gray, we are very much indebted to you. Thanks to you, we are out of debt, and shall have a balance of from twelve to fifteen dollars in the treasury."

"I am very glad of it," said Philip.

"So am I," said the professor, pushing forward, jealous lest Philip should get more than his share of credit.

"And we are indebted to you also, Professor Riccabocca," said the president, taking the hint.

"You are entirely welcome, sir," said Riccabocca loftily. "My help has often been asked in behalf of charitable organizations. I remember once, in Philadelphia, I alone raised five hundred dollars for a - a - I think it was a hospital."

This was an invention, but Professor Riccabocca had no scruple in getting up little fictions which he thought likely to redound to his credit and increase his reputation.

"Doubtless you are often called upon also, Mr. Gray," suggested Mr. Caswell with a smile.

"No," answered Philip. "This is the first time that I have ever had the opportunity."

"There's no humbug about the boy," thought Mr. Caswell. "As for the professor, he is full of it."

"I have pleasure in handing you the price agreed upon," said the president, presenting each with a ten-dollar bill.

"Thank you," said Philip.

Professor Riccabocca carelessly tucked the bill into his vest pocket, as if it were a mere trifle.

At this moment, Mr. Turner came up with all the other

gentleman. "Mr. Gray," he said, "here is a gentleman who wishes to speak to you."

Philip looked up, and saw the well-known figure of Squire Pope.

CHAPTER XXXVII.

HIS OWN MASTER.

"Ahem, Philip," said the squire. "I should like a little conversation with you."

"Good evening, Squire Pope," said our hero, not pretending to be cordial, but with suitable politeness.

"I didn't expect to see you here," pursued the squire.

"Nor I you, sir."

"I am visiting my sister, Mrs. Cunningham, who lives in Knoxville. Will you come around with me, and make a call?"

Now, considering the treatment which Philip had received from the squire before he left Norton, the reader can hardly feel surprised that our hero didn't care to trust himself with his unscrupulous fellow townsman.

"Thank you, Squire Pope," said Philip, "but it is rather late for me to call at a private house. I am staying at the hotel, and if you will take the trouble to go around there with me, we will have a chance to converse."

"Very well," said the squire, hesitating. Just then up came his niece, Carrie, who was determined to get acquainted with Philip.

"Uncle," she said, "introduce me to Mr. Gray."

"This is my niece, Caroline Cunningham," said the squire stiffly.

"I am glad to meet Miss Cunningham," said Philip, extending his hand, with a smile.

"What a lovely player you are, Mr. Gray!" she said impulsively.

"I am afraid you are flattering me, Miss Cunningham."

"Don't call me Miss Cunningham. My name is Carrie."

"Miss Carrie, then."

"I was ever so much surprised to hear that uncle was your guardian."

Philip looked quickly at the squire, but did not contradict it. He only said:

"We used to live in the same town."

During this conversation Squire Pope looked embarrassed and impatient.

"It's getting late, Carrie," he said. "You had better go home."

"Aren't you coming, too, uncle?"

"I am going to the hotel to settle some business with Philip."

"What business, I wonder?" thought our hero.

Arrived at the hotel, they went up-stairs to Philip's chamber. "You left Norton very abruptly, Philip," commenced the squire.

"There was good reason for it," answered Philip significantly.

"It appears to me you are acting as if you were your own master," observed the squire.

"I am my own master," replied Philip firmly.

"You seem to forget that I am your guardian."

"I don't forget it, for I never knew it," said our hero.

"It is generally understood that such is the case."

"I can't help it. I don't need a guardian, and shall get along without one."

"Ahem! Perhaps that isn't to be decided by you."

"If I am to have a guardian, Squire Pope," said Philip bluntly, "I sha'n't select you. I shall select Mr. Dunbar."

"I have much more knowledge of business than Mr. Dunbar," said the squire, shifting his ground.

"That may be, but there is one important objection."

"What is that?"

"You are not my friend, and Mr. Dunbar is."

"Really this is very extraordinary!" ejaculated the squire. "I am not your friend? How do you know that?"

"You tried to make a pauper out of me, when, as you must perceive, I am entirely able to earn my own living."

"Is it true that you were paid ten dollars for playing this evening?" asked the squire curiously.

"Yes, sir."

"It beats all!" said the squire, in amazement.

"Yet you wanted to sell my violin for a good deal less than I have earned in one evening," said Philip, enjoying his enemy's surprise.

"You gave an entertainment at Wilkesville also, I hear?"

"Yes, sir."

"Did you make as much there?"

"I made between sixty and seventy dollars over and above expenses."

"You don't expect me to believe that!" said the squire.

"I don't care whether you believe it or not; it's true."

"Have you got the money with you?"

"Yes."

"Then you'd better give it to me to keep for you."

"Thank you; I feel capable of taking care of it myself."

"But it's improper for a boy of your age to carry round so much money," said the squire sharply.

"If I need help to take care of it, I will ask Mr. Dunbar."

"Come, Philip," said the squire, condescending to assume a persuasive manner, "you must remember that I am your guardian."

"I dispute that," said Philip.

"I won't insist upon your going back with me to Norton, as long as you are able to support yourself."

"Then you wouldn't advise me to go back to the poorhouse," said Philip, with some sarcasm in his voice.

"I didn't mean to have you stay there long," said the squire, rather confused. "You'd better give me most of your money, and I'll take care of it for you, and when you're twenty-one you'll have quite a little sum.

"I am much obliged to you, sir, but I won't put you to the trouble of taking care of my money," answered Philip coldly.

Squire Pope continued to argue with Philip, but made no impression. At length he was obliged to say good night.

"I will call round in the morning," he said, at parting. "Perhaps you'll listen to reason then."

When he called round in the morning he learned to his disappointment that Philip was gone.

CHAPTER XXXVIII.

AN OFFER DECLINED.

After his interview with Squire Pope, Philip came down to the office, where he saw Professor Riccabocca, apparently waiting for him.

"Well, Mr. Gray, where shall we go next?" asked the professor, with suavity.

"I haven't decided where to go - have you?" asked Philip coolly.

"I suppose we had better go to Raymond. That is a good-sized place. I think we can get together a good audience there."

"You seem to be under the impression that we are in partnership," said Philip.

"Of course," answered Riccabocca.

"I have made no agreement of that sort, professor."

"But, of course, it is understood," said Riccabocca quickly, "as long as we draw so well."

"You must excuse me, Professor Riccabocca. I must

decline the proposal."

"But why?" inquired the professor anxiously.

"I hope you won't press me for an explanation."

"But I do. I can't understand why you should act so against your own interest. You can't expect people will come just to hear you play. You need me to help you."

"It may be as you say, professor, but if you insist upon my speaking plainly, I don't care to travel with a man who has treated me as you have."

"I don't understand you," said Riccabocca nervously; but it was evident, from his expression, that he did.

"Then you seem very forgetful," said Philip. "You tried to deprive me of my share of the proceeds of the entertainment at Wilkesville, and would have succeeded but for a lucky accident."

"I told you that it was all owing to neuralgia," said Professor Riccabocca. "I had such an attack of neuralgic headache that it nearly drove me wild."

"Then," said Philip, "I would rather find a partner who is not troubled with neuralgic headache. I think it would be safer."

"It won't happen again, Mr. Gray, I assure you," said the professor apologetically.

He endeavored to persuade Philip to renew the combination, but our hero steadily refused. He admitted that it might be to his pecuniary advantage, but he had lost all confidence in the eminent professor, and he thought it better to part now than to give him another opportunity of playing a similar trick upon him.

The professor thereupon consulted the landlord as to whether it would be advisable for him to give another entertainment unaided, and was assured very emphatically that it would not pay expenses.

"You make a great mistake, Mr. Gray," said Riccabocca. "It would be a great advantage for you to have my assistance at this stage of your professional career."

"I don't expect to have any professional career," answered Philip.

"Don't you intend to become a professional musician?" asked the professor, surprised.

"Probably not. I have only been playing because I needed money, and my violin helped me to a living."

"You can't make as much money in any other way."

"Not at present; but I want to get a chance to enter upon some kind of business. I am going to New York."

"You will some time have a chance to hear me there, in the Academy of Music," said Riccabocca pompously.

"I will go and hear you," said Philip, laughing, "if I can afford a ticket."

"Say the word and we will appear there together, Mr. Gray."

"I think not, professor."

In fact, though Philip had found himself unexpectedly successful as a musician, he knew very well that he was only a clever amateur, and that years of study would be needed to make him distinguished.

He was glad that he had the means of paying his expenses for a considerable time, and had in his violin a trusty friend upon which he could rely in case he got into financial trouble. Directly after breakfast he set out on his journey.

CHAPTER XXXIX.

AN AMBITIOUS WAYFARER.

The large sums which Philip had received for his playing might have dazzled a less sensible boy. He was quite conscious that he played unusually well for a boy, but when it came to selecting music as a profession, he felt it would not be wise to come to too hasty a decision. To be a commonplace performer did not seem to him very desirable, and would not have satisfied his ambition.

He had told Professor Riccabocca that he intended to go to New York. This design had not been hastily formed. He had heard a great deal of the great city in his home in the western part of the State of which it was the metropolis, and he was desirous of seeing it. Perhaps there might be some opening for him in its multitude of business houses.

Philip had plenty of money, and could easily have bought a railroad ticket, which would have landed him in New York inside of twenty-four hours, for he was only about four hundred miles distant; but he was in no hurry, and rather enjoyed traveling leisurely through the country towns, with his violin in his hand.

It reminded him of a biography he had read of the

Horatio Alger

famous Doctor Goldsmith, author of the "Vicar of Wakefield," who made a tour on the continent of Europe, paying his way with music evoked from a similar instrument.

Three days later, he found himself on the outskirts of a village, which I will call Cranston. It was afternoon, and he had walked far enough to be tired.

He was looking about for a pleasant place to lounge, when his attention was drawn to a boy of about his own age, who was sitting on the stone wall under a large tree.

He was rather a slender boy, and had originally been well dressed, but his suit was travel-stained, and covered with dust.

Now, boys have a natural attraction for each other, and Philip determined to introduce himself to the stranger. This he did in boy-fashion, by saying:

"Hello!"

"Hello!" said the stranger, looking up.

But he spoke slowly and wearily, and to Philip he seemed out of spirits.

"Do you live in Cranston?" asked Philip, taking a seat beside the other boy, upon the top of the stone wall.

"No; do you?"

"No."

"Where do you live?"

"I don't live anywhere just at present," answered Philip, with a smile. "I am traveling."

"So am I," said the other boy.

"I am traveling to New York," Philip continued.

"And I am traveling from there," said his new acquaintance.

Then both boys surveyed each other curiously.

"What's your name?" asked the stranger.

"Philip Gray. What's your's?"

"Mine is Henry Taylor. What have you got there?"

"A violin."

"Do you play on it?"

"Yes; a little."

"I should think you'd be tired lugging it round."

Philip smiled.

"It is about all the property I have," he said; "so it won't do for me to get tired of it."

"You're richer than I am, then," said Henry.

"Are you poor, then?" asked Philip, in a tone of sympathy.

"I haven't got a cent in my pocket, and I haven't had anything to eat since breakfast."

"Then I'm glad I met you," said Philip warmly. "I will see that you have a good supper. How long is it since you left New York?"

"About a week."

"What made you leave it?"

Henry Taylor hesitated, and finally answered, in a confused tone:

"I've run away from home. I wanted to go out West to kill Indians."

Philip stared at his new acquaintance in astonishment.

CHAPTER XL.

THE INDIAN HUNTER.

Philip had lived so long in a country village that he had never chanced to read any of those absorbing romances in which one boy, of tender years, proves himself a match for a dozen Indians, more or less, and, therefore, he was very much amazed at Henry Taylor's avowal that he was going out West to kill Indians.

"What do you want to kill Indians for?" he asked, after an astonished pause.

Now it was Henry's turn to be astonished.

"Every boy wants to kill Indians," he answered, looking pityingly at our hero.

"What for? What good will it do?" asked Philip.

"It shows he's brave," answered his new friend. "Didn't you ever read the story of 'Bully Bill'; or, The Hero of the Plains'?"

"I never heard of it," said Philip.

"You must have lived in the woods, then," said Henry Taylor, rather contemptuously. "It's a tip-top story.

Bully Bill was only fourteen, and killed ever so many Indians - twenty or thirty, I guess - as well as a lot of lions and bears. Oh, he must have had lots of fun!"

"Why didn't the Indians kill him?" asked Philip, desirous of being enlightened. "They didn't stand still and let him kill them, did they?"

"No; of course not. They fought awful hard."

"How did one young boy manage to overcome so many Indians?"

"Oh, you'll have to read the story to find out! Bully Bill was a great hero, and everybody admired him."

"So you wanted to imitate his example?" asked Philip.

"To be sure I did."

"How did you happen to get out of money?"

"Well," said Henry, "you see me and another boy got awful excited after reading the story, and both concluded nothing could make us so happy as to go out West together, and do as Bill did. Of course, it was no use to ask the old man -"

"The old man?" queried Philip.

"The gov'nor - father, of course! So we got hold of some money -"

"You got hold of some money?" queried Philip.

"That's what I said, didn't I?" rejoined Henry irritably.

"Yes."

"Then what's the use of repeating it?"

Philip intended to ask where or how Henry got hold of the money, but he saw pretty clearly that this would not be agreeable to his new acquaintance. Though without much experience in the world, he suspected that the money was not obtained honestly, and did not press the question.

"Well, me and Tom started about a week ago. First of all, we bought some revolvers, as, of course, we should need them to shoot Indians. They cost more than we expected, and then we found it cost more to travel than we thought."

"How much money did you have?"

"After paying for our revolvers, Tom and me had about thirty dollars," said Henry.

"Only thirty dollars to go west with!" exclaimed Philip, in amazement.

"Why, you see, the revolvers cost more than we expected. Then we stopped at a hotel in Albany, where they charged us frightfully. That is where Tom left me."

"Tom left you at Albany?"

"Yes, he got homesick!" said Henry contemptuously. "He thought we hadn't money enough, and he said he didn't know as he cared so much about killing Indians."

"I agree with Tom," said Philip. "I don't think I should care very much about killing Indians myself, and I should decidedly object to being killed by an Indian. I shouldn't like to be scalped. Would you?"

"Oh, I'd take care of that," said Henry. "I wouldn't let them have the chance."

"It seems to me the best way would be to stay at home," said Philip, smiling.

"If I stayed at home I'd have to go to school and study. I don't care much about studying."

"I like it," said Philip. "So Tom left you, did he?"

"Yes; but I wasn't going to give up so easy. He took half the money that was left, though I thought he ought to have given it to me, as I needed it more. I wasn't going home just as I'd started."

"Then you've spent all your money now?"

"Yes," answered Henry gloomily. "Have you got much money?" he asked, after a pause.

"Yes, I have about a hundred dollars-say, ninety-five."

"You don't mean it!" ejaculated Henry, hie eyes sparkling.

"Yes, I do."

"How did you get it?"

"I earned most of it by playing on the violin."

"I say," exclaimed Henry, in excitement, "suppose you and me go into partnership together, and go out West -"

"To kill Indians?" asked Philip, smiling.

"Yes! With all that money we'll get along. Besides, if we get short, you can earn some more."

"But what advantage am I to get out of it? I am to furnish all the capital and pay all expenses, as far as I can understand. Generally, both partners put in something."

"I put in my revolver," said Henry.

"One revolver won't do for us both."

"Oh, well, you can buy one. Come, what do you say?" asked Henry eagerly.

"Let me ask you a few questions first. Where does your father live?"

"In New York."

"What is his business?"

"He is a broker in Wall Street."

"I suppose he is rich?"

"Oh, he's got plenty of money, I expect! We live in a nice house on Madison Avenue. That's one of the best streets, I suppose you know!"

"I never was in New York. Is your mother living?"

"No," answered Henry. "She died three years ago."

If his mother had been living, probably the boy would never have made such an escapade, but his father, being engrossed by business cares, was able to give very little attention to his son, and this accounts in part for the folly of which he had been guilty.

"Have you got any brothers or sisters?" he asked.

"I have one sister, about three years younger than I. Her name is Jennie."

"I wish I were as well off as you," said Philip.

"How do you mean?"

"I mean I wish I had a father and sister."

"Haven't you?"

"My father is dead," said Philip gravely, "and I never had a sister."

"Oh, well, I don't know as I'm so lucky," said Henry. "Sisters are a bother. They want you to go round with them, and the old man is always finding fault."

Philip's relations with his father had always been so affectionate that he could not understand how Henry could talk in such a way of his.

"I don't know what makes you ask me such a lot of questions," said Henry, showing impatience. "Come, what do you say to my offer ?"

"About forming a partnership?"

"Yes."

"I'd rather not - in that way."

"In what way?"

"I mean for the purpose of going out West to kill Indians."

"You've no idea what fun it would be," said Henry, disappointed.

"No, I suppose not," said Philip, smiling.

"Then I suppose I shall have to give it up," said Henry.

"Now I have a proposal to make to you," said Philip.

"What is it?"

"If you agree to go home, I'll pay your expenses and go along with you. I've never been to New York, and I'd like to have some one with me that could show me round the city."

"I can do that," said Henry. "I know the way all about."

"Then will you agree?"

"Yes."

"Then come along, and we'll stop at the first convenient place and get some supper."

CHAPTER XLI.

AN ADVENTURE IN THE WOODS.

"I shall do a good thing if I induce Henry to go home," thought Philip. "That is rather a queer idea of his about wanting to kill Indians. It seems to me as much murder to kill an Indian as any one else."

He only thought this, but did not express it, as he did not care to get into a discussion with his new acquaintance, lest the latter should recall his consent to go home.

"I say, Philip," said Henry, who had now learned our hero's name, "we ain't in any hurry to go to New York, are we?"

"I thought we might take a train to-morrow morning, and go straight through."

"But I'd rather take it easy, and travel through the country, and have adventures."

"But you forget that your father will be anxious about you."

"Yes, I suppose he will."

"I'll tell you what I'll do. If you'll write a letter to your father, and let him know that you are safe with me, I'll do as you say."

"All right," said Henry, in a tone of satisfaction; "I'll do it."

"Father'll pay you all you have to spend for me," Henry added, after a moment's pause.

"Very well; then I will be your banker."

Philip was not foolish enough to protest that he did not care to be repaid. All he had in the world was a little less than a hundred dollars, and when that was gone he was not absolutely sure of making any more at once, though he felt tolerably confident that he could.

"Suppose you let me have ten dollars now," suggested Henry.

"I think I would rather keep the money and pay the bills," said Philip quietly.

He was not sure but that Henry, if he had a supply of money in his pockets, would reconsider his promise to go home and take French leave.

Of course, it would be extremely foolish, but his present expedition did not indicate the possession of much wisdom.

"I don't see what difference it makes," said Henry, looking dissatisfied.

"I won't argue the point," answered Philip good-naturedly.

"I wish I was in New York, near a good restaurant," said Henry, after a pause.

"Oh. I forgot! You are hungry."

"Awfully. I don't believe there's a hotel within two or three miles. I don't think I can hold out to walk much farther."

A few rods farther on was a farmhouse standing back from the road, old-fashioned-looking, but of comfortable aspect.

A young girl appeared at the side door and rang a noisy bell with great vigor.

"They're going to have supper," said Henry wistfully. "I wish it was a hotel!"

Philip had lived in the country, and understood the hospitable ways of country people.

"Come along, Henry," he said. "I'll ask them to sell us some supper. I am sure they will be willing."

Followed by his new acquaintance, he walked up to the side door and knocked - for there was no bell.

The young girl - probably about Philip's age - opened the door and regarded them with some surprise.

Philip bowed.

Horatio Alger

"Will you be kind enough to tell us if there is any hotel near-by?" he asked.

"There's one about three miles and a half farther on."

Henry groaned inwardly.

"I am going to ask you a favor," said Philip. "My friend and I have traveled a considerable distance, and stand in need of supper. We are willing to pay as much as we should have to at a hotel, if you will let us take supper here."

"I'll ask mother," said the young girl.

And forthwith she disappeared. She came back in company with a stout, motherly-looking woman. Philip repeated his request.

"Why, to be sure," she said heartily. "We always have enough, and to spare. Come right in, and we'll have supper as soon as the men-folks come in."

They entered a neat kitchen, in the middle of which was set out a table, with a savory supper upon it. Henry's eyes sparkled, and his mouth watered, for the poor boy was almost famished.

"If you want to wash come right in here," said the farmer's wife, leading the way into a small room adjoining.

The two boys gladly availed themselves of the permission, though Henry would not have minded sitting right down, dusty as he was. However, he felt better after he had washed his face and bands and wiped them on the long roll towel that hung beside the sink.

They were scarcely through, when their places were taken by the farmer and his son, the latter a tall, sun-burned young man, of about twenty, who had just come in from a distant field. The farmer's wife soon explained the presence of the two young strangers.

"Sho!" said the farmer. "You're pretty young to be travelin'. You ain't in any business, be you?"

Henry was rather ashamed to mention that his business was killing Indians, though, as yet, he had not done anything in that line. He had an idea that he might be laughed at.

"I am a little of a musician," said Philip modestly.

"Sho! do you make it pay?"

"Pretty well, so far; but I think when I get to New York I shall try something else."

"Are you a musician as well as he?" asked the farmer of Henry.

"No, sir."

"Come, father, you'd better sit down to supper, and do your talking afterward," said the farmer's wife.

So they sat down to the table, and all did full justice to the wholesome fare, particularly Henry, who felt absolutely ravenous.

Never at the luxurious home of his father, in Madison Avenue, had the wandering city boy enjoyed his supper as much as at the plain table of this country farmer.

The good mistress of the household was delighted at the justice done to her viands, considering it a tribute to her qualities as a cook.

When Philip produced his purse to pay for their supper, the farmer absolutely refused to receive anything. "But I would rather pay," persisted our hero.

"Then I'll tell you how you may pay. Give us one or two tunes on your violin."

This Philip was quite willing to do, and it is needless to say that his small audience was very much pleased.

"I say," said Henry, "you play well enough to give concerts."

"I have done it before now," answered Philip, smiling.

They were invited to spend the night, but desired to push on to the hotel, being refreshed by their supper and feeling able to walk three or four miles farther.

About half-way their attention was drawn to what appeared a deserted cabin in the edge of the woods, some twenty rods back from the road.

"I say, Philip," said Henry, "there's an old hut that looks as if nobody lived in it. Wouldn't it be a lark for us to sleep there to-night? It would save the expense of lodging at the hotel, and would be an adventure. I haven't had any adventures yet."

"I have no objection," said Philip. "We'll go, at any rate, and look at it."

They crossed the field, which seemed to have been only partially cleared, and soon reached the hut.

It was very bare within, but on the floor, in one corner, was a blanket spread out. There was a place for a window, but the sash had been removed, and it was easy to step in.

"I wonder how this blanket came here?" said Philip.

"Oh, I guess the last people that lived here left it!" returned Henry. "I say, Phil, I begin to feel tired. Suppose we lie down? I'm glad I haven't got to walk any farther."

Philip sympathized with his new friend; and so, without much parley, the two boys threw themselves down on the blanket, and were soon fast asleep.

How long Philip slept he didn't know, but he was awakened by a terrible screech, and, opening his eyes, say Henry sitting bolt upright, with trembling limbs and distended eyeballs, gazing fearfully at a tall, muscular-looking Indian, who had just stepped into the cabin through the open window.

CHAPTER XLII.

AN INDIAN AT LAST.

"What's the matter?" asked Philip, rubbing his eyes, for he was hardly able - so suddenly had he been roused from sleep - to comprehend the situation.

Henry, as white as a sheet, could only point at the tall Indian, who, standing motionless, was gazing as intently at the boys.

He made one step forward, and Henry thought he was about to be killed and scalped forthwith.

"Oh, Mr. Indian Chief," he exclaimed, in tremulous accents, "don't kill me! I - I ain't ready to die!"

The Indian looked amazed, and laughed gutturally, but did not speak. His laugh increased Henry's dismay.

"I've got a revolver. I'll give it to you if you won't kill me," continued Henry.

Then the Indian spoke.

"Why should I kill white boy?" he asked in a mild tone, which ought to have convinced Henry that he had nothing to fear.

But the boy was so frenzied with terror, and so possessed of the thought that the Indian was just like the savage warriors of the plains, of whom he had read so much, that he still felt his life to be in danger, and answered the question in a way not expected.

"I suppose you want my scalp," he said; "but I am only a boy, and I don't mean any harm. I hope you'll spare my life."

Another fit of guttural laughter from the Indian, which perplexed Henry, and after a pause he said:

"Me no want white boy's scalp! Me good Indian!"

An immense burden seemed lifted from poor Henry's breast.

"Then you don't want to kill me?" he said.

"No!"

"Then why do you come here?"

"Me live here."

The secret was out - a secret which Philip had suspected from the first, though Henry had not dreamed of it.

They had lain down in the Indian's cabin, appropriating his blanket, and were simply intruders.

Philip thought it was time for him to take part in the conversation,

"I hope you'll excuse us," he said, "for coming here. We had no idea any one lived here."

"No matter," said the Indian civilly - that being one of the phrases which his knowledge of English included.

"Henry," said Philip, "let us get up. We are sleeping in this - this gentleman's bed."

He felt a little at a loss how to designate the Indian, but felt that it was best to be as polite as possible.

The two boys started up, in order to yield to the master of the house the bed which properly belonged to him.

"No," said the Indian, with a wave of his hand. "White boys stay there. Indian sleep anywhere."

So saying, he lay down in one corner of the cabin, and settled himself apparently to repose.

"But," said Philip, "we don't want to take your bed."

"No matter!" said the Indian once more.

"You are very kind," said Philip. "Henry, we may as well lay down again."

Henry obeyed directions, but he was not altogether free from alarm. He had read that the Indians are very crafty. How did he know but their copper-colored host might get up in the night, skillfully remove their scalps, and leave them in a very uncomfortable plight?

"Hadn't we better get up, and run away as soon as he is asleep?" he whispered to Philip.

"No; he's friendly," answered Philip confidently.

As Henry had read about friendly Indians - all he knew about Indians, by the way, was derived from reading stories written by authors little wiser than himself - he concluded that perhaps there was nothing to fear, and after a while fell asleep again.

When the boys awoke it was morning. They looked toward the corner where the Indian had lain down, but it was vacant.

"He's gone." said Henry, rather relieved.

"You were pretty well frightened last night," said Philip, smiling.

"Who wouldn't be!" asked Henry; "to wake up and see a big Indian in the room?"

"I dare say many boys would be frightened," said Philip, "but I don't think a boy who left home to go out West to kill Indians ought to be afraid of one."

"I guess I'll give up going," said Henry, rather abashed.

"I think myself it would be as well," observed Philip quietly. "You'd find it rather serious business if you should meet any real Indian warriors."

"I don't know but I should," Henry admitted, rather awkwardly. "I didn't think much about it when I left home."

"I suppose you thought you'd be a match for half a dozen Indian warriors?" said Philip, laughing.

"That was the way with 'Bully Bill'; or, 'The Hero of the Plains,'" said Henry. "He always came off best when he fought with the Indians."

"I don't think either you or I will ever prove a Bully Bill," said Philip. "I might enjoy going out West some time, but I shouldn't expect to kill many Indians. I think they would stand a good deal better chance of shooting me."

Henry said nothing, but looked thoughtful. His romantic ideas seemed to have received a sudden shock, and he was trying to adjust his ideas to the new light he had received.

The boys were preparing to go out, when their Indian host suddenly reappeared. He carried in his hand a large-sized loaf of baker's bread, which he had procured at the village store. He was alive to the duties of hospitality, and did not intend to let his guests go, uninvited though they were, without a breakfast.

Though his stock of English was limited, he made out to invite the boys to breakfast with him.

Henry would have preferred to go to the hotel, but Philip signed to him to accept graciously the Indian's hospitality.

As the bread was fresh, they partook of it with relish, washing it down with drafts of clear spring water.

The Indian looked on, well pleased to see the justice done to his hospitality. He explained to the boys that he made baskets, caught fish, and sometimes engaged in hunting, managing, in one way and another, to satisfy his simple wants. His name was Winuca, but his white neighbors called him Tom.

When the boys were ready to go, Philip drew from his pocket a jack-knife, nearly new, of which he asked the Indian's acceptance.

Winuca seemed very much pleased, and shook hands heartily with his young guests, wishing them good-by.

The boys kept on to the hotel, where they spent a few hours, taking dinner there. Their breakfast had been so simple that they had a very good appetite for their midday meal.

"While we are here, Henry, suppose you write to your father and relieve his anxiety?" suggested Philip.

"Why can't you write?" asked Henry, who cherished the general boyish distaste for letter-writing.

"Because it will be more proper for you to write. I am a stranger to him."

"You won't be long, Philip? I shall want you to come and make me a visit."

"Perhaps you'll be tired of me before we get to New York," suggested Philip, with a smile.

"There isn't much chance of it. I like you better than any boy I know. You're awful brave, too. You didn't seem to be at all scared last night when the Indian came in."

"It was because I felt sure that any Indian to be found

about here would be harmless."

"I wish we could make a journey together some time. I'd like to go West -"

"To kill Indians?"

"No. If they'll let me alone, I'll let them alone; but there must be a lot of fun out on the prairies."

"Well, Henry, go and write your letter, and we can talk about that afterward."

The letter was written and mailed, and arrived in New York several days before the boys did.

CHAPTER XLIII.

A WELCOME LETTER.

Alexander Taylor, a Wall Street broker, sat at breakfast in his fine house on Madison Avenue. His daughter, Jennie, about thirteen years old, was the only other person at the table.

"Papa, have you heard nothing of Henry?" asked the little girl anxiously.

"Only that the boy who got started with him on his foolish tramp got back three days since."

"Is Tom Murray back, then?"

"Yes; he showed himself more sensible than Henry."

"Oh, I'm afraid something's happened to him, papa! Why don't you advertise for him, or send out a detective, or something?"

"I will tell you, Jennie," said Mr. Taylor, laying down the morning paper. "I want your brother to stay away long enough to see his folly."

"But perhaps he may get out of money, and not be able to get anything to eat. You wouldn't want him to starve, papa?"

"There isn't much chance of it. If he is in danger of that, he will have sense enough to ask for food, or to write to me for help. I rather hope he will have a hard time."

"Oh, papa!"

"It will do him good. If I sent for him and brought him back against his will, he would probably start off again when he has a good chance."

Jennie could not quite follow her father in his reasoning, and was inclined to think him hard and unfeeling. She missed her brother, who, whatever his faults, treated her tolerably well, and was at any rate a good deal of company, being the only other young person in the house.

Just then the servant entered with three letters, which he laid down beside his master's plate.

Mr. Taylor hastily scanned the addresses.

"Here is a letter from Henry," he said, in a tone of satisfaction.

"Oh, read it quick, papa!"

This was the letter which Mr. Taylor read aloud, almost too deliberately for the impatience of his daughter:

"Dear Father: I am alive and well, and hope to see you in a few days. I guess I made a mistake in running away, though I didn't think so at the time, for I wanted to see life, and have adventures. I don't know how I should have got along if I hadn't met Philip Gray. He's a tip-top fellow, and is paying my expenses. I told him you would pay him back. He has got me off the idea of going West to kill Indians."

"Oh, papa!" exclaimed Jennie, opening her eyes wide. "I didn't know that was what Henry went for."

"I don't think the Indians would have felt very much frightened if they had heard of his intention. However, I will proceed:

"I was all out of money when Philip met me, and I hadn't had anything to eat since morning, he bought me some supper, and is paying my expenses. He is a poor boy, coming to New York to get a place, if he can. He has got a violin, and he plays beautifully. He earned all the money he has by giving concerts."

"I should like to see Philip," said Jennie, with interest.

"I asked him if he wouldn't go out West with me, but he wouldn't. He told me he wouldn't do anything for me unless I would agree to come home."

"He is a sensible boy," commented Mr. Taylor, in a tone of approval.

"We thought at first of coming right home on the cars, but I wanted to walk and see something of the country, and Philip said he didn't mind. He told me I must write and tell you, so that you needn't feel anxious.

"You will see us in a few days. I will bring

Philip to the house. Your son, HENRY TAYLOR."

"Is that all?" asked Jennie.

"Yes; I consider it a very fair letter. It is evident Henry has made the acquaintance of a sensible boy. I shall take care that he doesn't let it drop."

CHAPTER XLIV.

A FRESH START.

Five days later, just as Mr. Tayior was sitting down to dinner, at the close of the day, the door-bell rang violently.

There was a hurried step heard in the hall, and the door opening quickly Henry Taylor rushed in, his face beaming with smiles.

"Oh, I'm so glad to see you, Henry!" said Jennie, embracing him. "I missed you awfully."

Henry looked at his father, a little doubtful of his reception.

"Are you well, father?" he asked.

"Quite well," responded Mr. Taylor coolly. "Where did you leave your scalps?"

"What?" ejaculated Henry, bewildered.

"I thought you left home to kill Indians."

"Oh!" said Henry, smiling faintly. "I didn't meet any Indians - except one - and he was friendly."

"Then your expedition was a failure?"

"I guess I'll leave the Indians alone," said Henry sheepishly.

"That strikes me as a sensible remark. Of course, a few Indian scalps would be of great use to you. I fully expected a present of one, as a trophy of my son's valor; but still, in case the Indian objected to being scalped, there might be a little risk in performing the operation."

"I see you are laughing at me, father," said Henry.

"Not at all. You can see that I am very sober. If you think you can make a good living hunting Indians - I don't know myself how much their scalps bring in the market - I might set you up in the business."

"I am not so foolish as I was. I prefer some other business. Philip told me -"

"Where is Philip?" asked Jennie eagerly.

"I left him in the parlor. He said I had better come in first."

"Go and call him. Invite him, with my compliments, to stay to dinner."

Henry left the room, and reappeared almost immediately with Philip.

Both boys were perfectly neat in appearance, for Philip had insisted on going to a hotel and washing and dressing themselves.

As he followed Henry into the room, with modest self-possession, his cheeks glowing with a healthy color, both Jennie and Mr. Taylor were instantly prepossessed in his favor.

"I am glad to see you, Philip," said the broker, "and beg to thank you, not only for the material help you gave Henry, but also for the good advice, which I consider of still greater importance and value."

"Thank you, sir. I don't feel competent to give much advice, but I thought his best course was to come home."

"You haven't as high an idea of hunting Indians as Henry, I infer?"

"No, sir," answered Philip, smiling. "It seems to me they have as much right to live as we, if they behave themselves."

"I think so, too," said Henry, who was rather ashamed of what had once been his great ambition.

"You haven't introduced me to Philip - I mean Mr. Gray," said Jennie.

"This is my sister Jennie, Phil," said Henry, in an off-hand manner.

"I am very glad to see you, Mr. Gray," said Jennie, extending her hand.

"I am hardly used to that name," said Philip, smiling.

"When I get well acquainted with you I shall call

you Philip."

"I hope you will."

Within an hour Miss Jennie appeared to feel well acquainted with her brother's friend, for she dropped "Mr. Gray" altogether, and called him Philip.

At her solicitation he played on his violin. Both Mr. Taylor and Jennie were surprised at the excellence of his execution.

When Philip rose to go, Mr. Taylor said cordially:

"I cannot permit you to leave us, Philip. You must remain here as our guest."

"But, sir, I left my things at a hotel."

"Then Henry will go with you and get them."

So Philip found himself established in a fine house on Madison Avenue as a favored guest.

The next morning, when Mr. Taylor went to his office, he asked Philip to go with him. Arrived in Wall Street, he sent a boy to the bank with a check. On his return, he selected five twenty-dollar bills, and handed them to Philip.

"You have expended some money for Henry," he said.

"Yes, sir; but not quarter as much as this."

"Then accept the rest as a gift. You will probably need some new clothes. Henry will take you to our tailor.

Don't spare expense. The bill will be sent to me."

"But, Mr. Taylor, I do not deserve such kindness."

"Let me be the judge of that. In a few days I shall have a proposal to make to you."

This was the proposal, and the way it was made:

"I find, Philip," said Mr. Taylor, some days later, "that Henry is much attached to you, and that your influence over him is excellent. He has agreed to go to an academy in Connecticut, and study hard for a year, provided you will go with him. I take it for granted you haven't completed your education?"

"No, sir."

"I shall pay all the bills and provide for you in every way, exactly as I do for Henry."

"But, Mr. Taylor, how can I ever repay you?" asked Philip.

"By being Henry's friend and adviser - perhaps, I may say, guardian - for, although you are about the same age, you are far wiser and more judicious."

"I will certainly do the best I can for him, sir."

During the next week the two boys left New York, and became pupils at Doctor Shelley's private academy, at Elmwood - a pleasant country town not far from Long Island Sound - and there we bid them adieu.

Choose from Thousands of 1stWorldLibrary Classics By

Adolphus WilliamWard
Aesop
Agatha Christie
Alexander Aaronsohn
Alexander Kielland
Alexandre Dumas
Alfred Gatty
Alfred Ollivant
Alice Duer Miller
Alice Turner Curtis
Alice Dunbar
Ambrose Bierce
Amelia E. Barr
Andrew Lang
Andrew McFarland Davis
Anna Sewell
Annie Besant
Annie Hamilton Donnell
Annie Payson Call
Anton Chekhov
Arnold Bennett
Arthur Conan Doyle
Arthur Ransome
Atticus
B. M. Bower
Basil King
Bayard Taylor
Ben Macomber
Booth Tarkington
Bram Stoker
C. Collodi
C. E. Orr
C. M. Ingleby
Carolyn Wells
Catherine Parr Traill
Charles A. Eastman
Charles Dickens
Charles Dudley Warner
Charles Farrar Browne
Charles Ives
Charles Kingsley
Charles Lathrop Pack
Charles Whibley
Charles Willing Beale
Charlotte M. Braeme
Charlotte M.Yonge
Clair W. Hayes
Clarence Day Jr.
Clarence E. Mulford

Clemence Housman
Confucius
Cornelis DeWitt Wilcox
Cyril Burleigh
D. H. Lawrence
Daniel Defoe
David Garnett
Don Carlos Janes
Donald Keyhole
Dorothy Kilner
Dougan Clark
E. Nesbit
E.P.Roe
E. Phillips Oppenheim
Edgar Allan Poe
Edgar Rice Burroughs
Edith Wharton
Edward J. O'Biren
John Cournos
Edwin L. Arnold
Eleanor Atkins
Elizabeth Cleghorn
Gaskell
Elizabeth Von Arnim
Ellem Key
Emily Dickinson
Erasmus W. Jones
Ernie Howard Pie
Ethel Turner
Ethel Watts Mumford
Eugenie Foa
Eugene Wood
Evelyn Everett-Green
Everard Cotes
F. J. Cross
Federick Austin Ogg
Ferdinand Ossendowski
Francis Bacon
Francis Darwin
Frances Hodgson Burnett
Frank Gee Patchin
Frank Harris
Frank Jewett Mather
Frank L. Packard
Frederick Trevor Hill
Frederick Winslow Taylor
Friedrich Kerst
Friedrich Nietzsche
Fyodor Dostoyevsky

Gabrielle E. Jackson
Garrett P. Serviss
Gaston Leroux
George Ade
Geroge Bernard Shaw
George Ebers
George Eliot
George MacDonald
George Orwell
George Tucker
George W. Cable
George Wharton James
Gertrude Atherton
Grace E. King
Grant Allen
Guillermo A. Sherwell
Gulielma Zollinger
Gustav Flaubert
H. A. Cody
H. B. Irving
H. G. Wells
H. H. Munro
H. Irving Hancock
H. Rider Haggard
H. W. C. Davis
Hamilton Wright Mabie
Hans Christian Andersen
Harold Avery
Harold McGrath
Harriet Beecher Stowe
Harry Houidini
Helent Hunt Jackson
Helen Nicolay
Hendy David Thoreau
Henrik Ibsen
Henry Adams
Henry Ford
Henry Frost
Henry James
Henry Jones Ford
Henry Seton Merriman
Henry Wadsworth
Longfellow
Henry W Longfellow
Herbert A. Giles
Herbert N. Casson
Herman Hesse
Homer
Honore De Balzac

Horace Walpole
Horatio Alger, Jr.
Howard Pyle
Howard R. Garis
Hugh Lofting
Hugh Walpole
Humphry Ward
Ian Maclaren
Israel Abrahams
J.G.Austin
J. Henri Fabre
J. M. Barrie
J. Macdonald Oxley
J. S. Knowles
J. Storer Clouston
Jack London
Jacob Abbott
James Allen
James Lane Allen
James Andrews
James Baldwin
James DeMille
James Joyce
James Oliver Curwood
James Oppenheim
James Otis
Jane Austen
Jens Peter Jacobsen
Jerome K. Jerome
John Burroughs
John F. Kennedy
John Gay
John Glasworthy
John Habberton
John Joy Bell
John Milton
John Philip Sousa
Jonathan Swift
Joseph Carey
Joseph Conrad
Joseph Jacobs
Julian Hawthrone
Julies Vernes
Justin Huntly McCarthy
Kakuzo Okakura
Kenneth Grahame
Kate Langley Bosher
L. A. Abbot
L. T. Meade
L. Frank Baum
Laura Lee Hope

Laurence Housman
Leo Tolstoy
Leonid Andreyev
Lewis Carroll
Lilian Bell
Lloyd Osbourne
Louis Tracy
Louisa May Alcott
Lucy Fitch Perkins
Lucy Maud Montgomery
Lydia Miller Middleton
Lyndon Orr
M. H. Adams
Margaret E. Sangster
Margaret Vandercook
Maria Edgeworth
Maria Thompson Daviess
Mariano Azuela
Marion Polk Angellotti
Mark Overton
Mark Twain
Mary Austin
Mary Cole
Mary Rowlandson
Mary Wollstonecraft
Shelley
Max Beerbohm
Myra Kelly
Nathaniel Hawthrone
O. F. Walton
Oscar Wilde
Owen Johnson
P.G.Wodehouse
Paul and Mable Thorn
Paul G. Tomlinson
Paul Severing
Peter B. Kyne
Plato
R. Derby Holmes
R. L. Stevenson
Rabindranath Tagore
Rahul Alvares
Ralph Waldo Emmerson
Rene Descartes
Rex E. Beach
Richard Harding Davis
Richard Jefferies
Robert Barr
Robert Frost
Robert Gordon Anderson
Robert L. Drake

Robert Lansing
Robert Michael Ballantyne
Robert W. Chambers
Rosa Nouchette Carey
Ross Kay
Rudyard Kipling
Samuel B. Allison
Samuel Hopkins Adams
Sarah Bernhardt
Selma Lagerlof
Sherwood Anderson
Sigmund Freud
Standish O'Grady
Stanley Weyman
Stella Benson
Stephen Crane
Stewart Edward White
Stijn Streuvels
Swami Abhedananda
Swami Parmananda
T. S. Ackland
The Princess Der Ling
Thomas A. Janvier
Thomas A Kempis
Thomas Anderton
Thomas Bailey Aldrich
Thomas Bulfinch
Thomas De Quincey
Thomas H. Huxley
Thomas Hardy
Thomas More
Thornton W. Burgess
U. S. Grant
Valentine Williams
Victor Appleton
Virginia Woolf
Walter Scott
Washington Irving
Wilbur Lawton
Wilkie Collins
Willa Cather
Willard F. Baker
William Makepeace
Thackeray
William W. Walter
Winston Churchill
Yei Theodora Ozaki
Young E. Allison
Zane Grey

www.ingramcontent.com/pod-product-compliance
Lightning Source LLC
Chambersburg PA
CBHW021335250626
47155CB00002B/710